MARKED FOR MAYHEM

SUSAN HAYES

Copyright © 2022 Susan Hayes

Marked For Mayhem (Book one of the Crashed and Claimed series)

First print Publication: March 2022

Editor: Amanda Brown

Cover Art: Croco Designs

Published by: Black Scroll Publications Ltd

ABOUT THE BOOK

**Her last shot at love just crashed and burned...
literally.**

Bella signed up for the interplanetary courtship cruise
hoping for travel, adventure, and maybe a chance at
romance. Now she's crash landed on a strange planet with
no one around but a horned alien hottie who showed up
and laid claim to her gear, her ship... and *her*.

He's too brash, too pushy, and much too young for her. He's
also not taking no for an answer...

This wasn't the adventure she imagined, but it might be the
romance of a lifetime, if she can stay alive long enough to
enjoy it.

***Buckle up. This sci-fi romance contains an alien with fur,
fangs, horns, and a very possessive attitude when it comes to*

1

"This was *not* in the brochure," Bella muttered as she clung to the straps of her safety harness. She kept her eyes tightly closed as she spent what she assumed were the last minutes of her life trying to pin down which of her many dubious choices had led her astray.

The escape pod pitched and shook as it plummeted toward the surface at speeds she didn't want to contemplate. If the thrusters failed, there'd be nothing left but a crater and a schmear of organic goo that had once been Bella-shaped.

She decided that signing up for the galactic matchmaking cruise had been the key mistake. What was she thinking, looking for love at her age? It didn't matter what species they were. Males were all the same. They wanted someone young and pretty to warm their bed and boost their ego, and while Bella had been young once, she'd never been pretty.

She heard her father's voice in her head, exactly the same as it had been the day he'd called her into the front room and laid out his plans for her future. "You're a handsome woman, Bella, but you'll never be beautiful. Beauty offers its own kind of power, but you're not destined for that. You're going to have to find other ways to get by in life. I've got no money or power of my own, but I know men who have both. The best I can do for you is to give you to one of them. You'll have to make your own way after that."

She'd taken her father's advice and gone with the man he'd chosen for her, a crime lord named Felix Natar. Maybe that had been a mistake, too, but she'd had limited options back then.

The same could be said for her current situation. She'd traveled from planet to planet, watching as the other women made their choices and left for their new lives. Now only a handful of them remained, rattling around the lushly appointed ship like loose change in a rich man's purse. At least, they had been... before it had all gone to the nine hells.

One minute they were zipping along in hyperspace, and the next the ship convulsed and shuddered as something that felt like a shock wave tore through it. After that, there'd been nothing but chaos.

The captain had come on, shouting orders Bella barely heard over the alarms that screeched and wailed from every speaker. Heavy, airtight doors slammed shut, sealing off various compartments.

Bella tried to remember the drills they'd all been put through at the start of the cruise. Emergency procedures. She needed to be somewhere right now... *Shit*! The escape pods.

She was only halfway to the nearest evac station when

something loud happened and the ship rocked again, throwing her to her knees.

She was barely on her feet again before a new, even louder klaxon sounded and every monitor in view lit up bright red, all flashing the same message in various languages. "Abandon Ship."

She'd followed the flashing arrows to the nearest escape pod and strapped herself into the one-man vessel. The moment she had her harness fastened, the door sealed, and she'd been ejected into space.

An annoyingly calm, automated voice came on within seconds of launch while Bella was still dealing with the sudden loss of gravity. The voice announced the pod would attempt to land on the nearest planet and began reciting instructions pertaining to various crash scenarios. "In case of a water landing..."

Bella ignored it. She had no idea what the surface looked like. It could be water, land, or molten rock, for all she knew. She didn't even know *where* they were. All she had to go on was what little information scrolled across the pod's single monitor. The planet had a breathable atmosphere, multiple healthy ecosystems, and not much else. No cities. No ports. No datasphere. She couldn't even see what it looked like. The pod had no windows, and the monitor kept scrolling the same few lines of text. All she could do was hold on and hope.

Laughter bubbled up in giddy giggles that morphed into maniacal gales. She was about to crash land on a strange planet and probably die there... This was so not the way she imagined this cruise ending for her.

Bella didn't remember the moment of impact. One second she'd been laughing like a lunatic, and the next thing she knew, she was staggering through the open door of her pod, coughing up the suspension gel that must have been triggered while she was still airborne.

The gel had saved her life, but holy hells, it reeked. She hacked and spat as much of the vile crap out of her body as she could, her attempts to clear her mouth and lungs triggering several rounds of nausea as her much-abused stomach got in on the action. Once her insides were dealt with, she switched her attention to the outside.

"Fuck." She was drenched in the snot-slick stuff and more was oozing out of the pod. A goopy pool of it gathered around the open door, making the scorched ground sizzle and hiss anywhere the liquid touched.

Scorched ground. Right. So, the thrusters had kicked in like they were supposed to. She was still dizzy enough that falling back into the goop was a risk, so she moved a few meters away. Once she found a patch of reasonably clear ground, she planted her feet and took her first look around.

Trees. That was her first impression. She'd crashed into a forest of some kind. The ground was thick with a spongy carpet she assumed was some kind of moss, though it was a far cry from the blue-green stuff she'd seen before. This was a burnt orange color, though it looked to be healthy enough. The trees overhead had foliage of similar shades. Reds and oranges with a few splashes of gold here and there. She couldn't smell much over the cloying smell of the goop, but the air was definitely breathable.

The second that thought popped into her head, she tossed it right back out again. Obviously, it was breathable. She'd have suffocated by now otherwise. Fortunately, the cruise came with a health package that had provided the women with all sorts of boosters to help them acclimatize to different oxygen levels and immunize them against dozens of pathogens and parasites. Handy when they were being toured around the galaxy looking for love... and damned useful now she was on a strange planet.

Whatever wound up killing her would have to be bigger than a virus. She looked around warily. "That was not an invitation for anything to try and kill me right now. In fact, I'd recommend waiting until I've gotten this crap off me first. Trust me, it does not taste good."

She sank down on a moss-covered stone, gathered up a handful of the thick, orange stuff, and used it to scrub the worst of the gunk off herself.

Over the next few minutes, the natural sounds of the wood returned as whatever wildlife called this place home got over the shock of her sudden and noisy arrival. The pod had torn a path through the canopy, snapping off branches as it plowed through on its way to the ground. Sunlight poured through the gap, and after a few more minutes, she opted to move to a shadier spot. The sun was baking the remaining gel into a hard, tacky mess that itched.

She wanted to find a nice pool of water somewhere and clean up, but that couldn't be her first priority. Being clean was a luxury. Shelter, food, and drinkable water were necessities. She eyed the pod that had brought her here. It was oblong, windowless, and a little worse for wear after atmospheric re-entry and the beating it took from the local plant life. Plus, the inside was coated in slowly dissolving goo.

Whoever had designed these things clearly didn't intend for the pod to act as any kind of shelter once it was on the ground. Of course, most times escape pods would drift around in space and wait for rescue. The space-to-planet ratio was heavily skewed toward the empty space side of the scale.

Still, it was better than nothing. And hadn't that stupid voice mentioned something about emergency supplies at some point during the descent?

She crossed over to the still-cooling pod and took a closer look. There! Near the bottom, she spotted a panel marked in multiple languages. She couldn't read them all—her translators only worked on spoken speech, not written words—but the ones she could make out all said the same thing. "Emergency kit inside."

The metal was still hot, but she managed to get the panel open without burning herself. She found two containers inside. One was marked as rations and the other as an emergency shelter. She grabbed them both and lugged them over to the shady rock she'd used earlier. At least, that's what she tried to do. The reality was something quite different.

The containers were heavy and awkward, and the thick moss made it almost impossible to pick her way through the uneven footing. After just a few steps she tripped over something and stumbled, dropping both items in the process.

Before she could recover her balance, she was deafened

by an explosive whooshing noise and something hit her in the back, knocking her off her feet.

The moss was soft, but the roots and rocks she landed on weren't. *Ow.*

She'd fallen too many times in her life to make the mistake of moving before she was certain nothing was broken. It only took a few seconds to determine she had a few bruises and scrapes but nothing more serious. Good enough.

Time to see what the hell had knocked her down and made that hideous noise. She got awkwardly to her feet, grateful no one could see her right now. Then she looked behind her. Something large and yellow was caught between the trunks of several trees. It shuddered and hissed like a suitcase full of unhappy snakes, and it took Bella's scattered senses a few seconds to work out what had happened. Her shelter had attacked her.

She looked on in dismay as the large inflatable structure slowly deflated through several freshly torn holes. She'd somehow managed to activate it when she stumbled. It had inflated and then rapidly run out of room since it was far too big to fit into the densely treed space. The rocks and branches had torn holes in it, and now it was dying a sad, leaky death as she watched.

Fucking hells. Even if she found a patch kit, it couldn't possibly be extensive enough to fix all the leaks, and she didn't see anywhere nearby to set it up if she did. The shelter was useless.

At least she still had the rest of the supplies. Maybe she could cut up the shelter to make a tarp or something. If she could find something to cut it with. She needed something to defend herself with, too, because anywhere as lush and full as life as this spot had to have wildlife in abundance.

"Something here is going to try to eat me. I just know it."

Movement out of the corner of her eye made her spin around. Some kind of serpent-like creature had come up behind her, its red and orange coloring helping it blend into the forest floor.

Bella had no idea if it was dangerous or not, but she wasn't about to take that chance. She slowly lifted one foot off the ground and eased her shoe off. It was a sensible flat, durable and comfortable.

She took aim and hurled it at the creature's head. Her throw was off, but it was enough to make the serpent veer off and then turn to slither back into the forest.

"Something might eat me eventually," she called after the snake as she limped over to pick up her shoe, "but it won't be you."

2

TODAY WAS one of the slow, sultry days Mayhem both loved and hated. He'd been on this planet long enough to be used to the heat, but the warmth and quiet always tempted him to take a few hours to relax and doze in a hammock somewhere with a breeze and a cool drink. That was the problem. No matter how tempting, he had too many things to do to take time away from work.

At least this job would be done soon. It would have taken him more than week to tackle alone, but two of his clansmen had come over to help. Between the three of them, it would take a day or two at most. Then, he'd return the favor. They all preferred to live separately, but they were still a clan. If they didn't help each other, none of them would survive.

He glanced up at the sky. Overhead, everything was bright and clear, but clouds were gathering on the horizon. Another storm was brewing, and in a few months, the rainy season would be here again.

He and the others had endured it their first year on the

planet, but this time they'd be better prepared. They were all busy improving their homes and honing their new skills. The fa'rel weren't a big group. Their creators had limited their numbers to ensure they could maintain control of their subjects, and he'd lost several of his brothers in the events leading up to their arrival on this planet.

A handful of them had lost their lives afterward, either to hostile lifeforms or natural threats like the flash floods that accompanied the first heavy rains. Those who remained had mourned their dead, learned new lessons, and kept their departed brothers alive by sharing memories of who they'd been and what they'd done when they were alive.

One day, no one would be left to tell those stories. None of them knew how long they'd live, but even if their lives could be measured in centuries, it wouldn't matter. They were alone on this world. Their creators, a species called the verexi, ensured that no one ever came here, and no one on the planet was allowed to leave. The verexi claimed it was for their creations' protection, but Mayhem and the others knew better. They weren't being protected. They were prisoners. The verexi hadn't let them go. They'd only given them a bigger prison—and they hadn't done it willingly.

Remembering how they'd gotten here stirred old angers, and that made him careless.

He nearly ruined an hour's work by yanking too hard at the dried grass he was trying to weave into the roof of his newly expanded home. The main area was shielded by scavenged pieces of the ship they'd arrived in, but they had a limited supply of that metal, far too small for all of them to use it to expand their homes. Instead, they'd all agreed to use local materials for any extensions and new buildings, using trial and error to find what worked best. Bysshe scoured what was left of the ship's databases to learn what he could, but most of it they had to work out for themselves.

"If you fuck that up, you can fix it yourself," Menace said. He was working on the same part of the roof as Mayhem but from below.

"You grumble more than Strife when it rains. It's fine," Mayhem retorted.

Menace stared up at him through the partially finished roof, his golden eyes narrowed. "No need to be insulting. I don't grumble anywhere near as much as he does."

Strife wasn't in sight, but apparently he was within earshot. He uttered an annoyed snarl, and a moment later they were both caught in a sudden shower of the thin, pliant branches Strife had been gathering from the trees above.

By the time the air was clear, Strife had vanished, though he could follow the other male's passage by the sounds he made as he bounded up into the canopy again, accompanied by a light riff of laughter.

"Asshole!" Menace hollered at Strife. "Now we need to stop and clean up this mess before we can start the next section."

"You're grumbling again," Mayhem said.

"One more comment from you and I'm going home. You can finish this yourself."

Mayhem didn't reply. He knew it was an empty threat. Bickering was how they eased the tension that always came when they spent more than a few hours in each other's company. It wasn't that they disliked each other. They cared for each other like family. Or at least, how he imagined a family would be. They all wanted to be in control of every situation, and that wasn't possible when they came together.

Bysshe was the only one who didn't feel that way. As an android, he didn't seem to feel much of anything. He was the calm, sensible one they all trusted and listened to.

Thinking about the android reminded him that he needed to visit Bysshe soon. Like the rest of them, the android lived alone. Unlike the others, though, he'd chosen to stay at the original crash site. He'd transformed the wreckage into something that benefited the entire clan, of which he was an honorary, but vital, member.

Bysshe had been the one to warn them of the verexi's plans, and he'd helped them overcome the ship's robotic crew. Without him, they'd all be dead. They owed him everything, but all he'd asked for was their friendship.

It was an easy bargain to make.

A strident series of beeps shattered the still afternoon and Mayhem swung down from the half-finished roof with a curse. Either a meteor was headed their way, or the verexi were about to try and finish the job of destroying their creations... again.

He dropped lightly to the main floor and made straight for the small room that housed his collection of salvaged ship components. It wasn't much, but with Bysshe's help and training they'd managed to cobble together a simple system that could detect anything that tried to fly into the area the fa'rel had claimed. Menace joined him, and a few seconds later Strife did, too. He landed with a thump and moved in behind Menace, the two of them blocking out most of the light that came through the door.

"What is it?" Menace asked.

One look at the monitor confirmed what he'd suspected.

"We're about to have company," he told them.

Both of them snarled. They knew what that meant. Mayhem moved to one side so they could both see the monitor. What looked like one main ship and several much smaller ones were visible. It looked like one would land in the area he'd claimed while two others were on trajectories that would take them into Menace and Strife's territories. The main ship looked like it would land some distance away, on the far side of a range of hills.

"Why land their main force there?" Strife asked.

Mayhem shook his head. The tactics didn't make sense to him either. "Maybe the scrawnies warned whoever it is that we're hard to kill and they're trying something different."

Strife snarled. "It won't work."

"When will they stop trying?" Menace asked angrily.

Mayhem turned, his expression hard. "Let them come. This is our home and we'll defend it."

"To the death," Strife added.

"To the death," Menace repeated.

The three of them butted heads, their horns clacking as they touched. "Good hunting," Mayhem told his brothers.

They nodded once and bounded over the railing. They would both have to return to their own homes to gear up before they could track down the invaders in their territory. If he hurried, he could claim first kill of the hunt.

It took only seconds to don his hunting gear and gather an array of weapons. They were all blades and spears he'd crafted himself. What few energy weapons they'd scavenged were stored in remains of the crashed ship, all carefully maintained and guarded by Bysshe for the day the enemy came in force. Until then, he and the others only used basic weapons. Besides, it made things more sporting. The fa'rel were created to be weapons of war. They only needed the skills and abilities they were born with to fulfill their purpose in life. They were hunters. Killers. Soldiers.

He stepped onto the veranda of his home, grabbed the signal gun that hung on the wall, and fired it past the canopy of trees to the clear air beyond. Bright green light and smoke poured from flare accompanied by an ear-piercing screech that would draw the attention of all his brothers.

They'd hear the warning and know a hunt was in progress. None of the others had equipment capable of tracking incoming ships, so they relied on him to watch the skies and send warnings. Now he'd done that task, it was time to go hunting.

He leapt from the deck of his home into the branches below, using his claws to catch hold of each limb and adding fresh gouge marks to the others that already scarred the bark. He bounded back and forth, each jump taking him closer to the ground.

The second he touched down, he was off and running, navigating the dense forest by memory occasionally aided by marks notched into the trees along his preferred routes. The forest floor was covered in thick moss and underbrush that didn't give way easily to the passage of animals, so they'd learned to mark the trees instead of looking for trails to follow.

Mayhem ran at a steady lope, vaulting over fallen logs

and root-tangled rocks. He moved quietly with only the occasional slide of a loose stone or crack of a dead twig announcing his presence. After a year, even the animals of the forest recognized him as one of their own. Potential prey went quiet and still when they sensed him, but the rest continued their lives unconcerned. The local varieties of pollinators buzzed and droned around him as lizards and avian-like creatures warbled and called to each other from their perches high in the canopy that stretched out overhead like a second sky.

This was the freedom Mayhem had dreamed of. No walls. No locked doors. No cold-eyed, spindle-limbed verexi watching from behind thick glass as he'd been tested on and mutilated in the name of knowledge.

He would never go back to that life. Never. It wasn't a perfect life, but it was *his*. Now he was free, he'd do all he could to stay that way and ensure his clansman, his brothers, stayed free, too.

He kept running until the scent of scorched wood and dirt tickled his nose, warning him that he was close. Strange, he'd expected them to land in one of the clearings that dotted the area, but they'd come down in the heart of the forest.

Something about that felt wrong, but he'd worry about their tactics once he'd seen who, and what, he was up against. The verexi never fought their own battles. They were so physically frail that the fa'rel called them "scrawnies."

But only when they were certain they couldn't be overheard.

Rage had been the first to come up with the name, and

the others had adopted it. Rage had been the unofficial leader of their clan—the eldest and the only survivor of the verexi's first attempts to create a race of super soldiers. He'd been there for every part of their imprisonment. Well, every part except their escape. He'd been dead by then. The scrawnies had killed him as a warning to the others to stop trying to escape. At least, that's what they'd been told, but they'd never seen their brother's body and neither had Bysshe. Part of him hoped that meant the verexi had lied, and Rage was alive somewhere. He knew the odds were against it, but he held on to the hope anyway.

If Rage were here, he'd snarl, cuff him upside the head, and tell him to stop being stupid.

"Don't feel. Act." He could almost hear the other male's voice beside him as he ran. "Feelings are a luxury we can't afford."

"Fuck that. Now that we're free, I can afford to feel. I'm dedicating this hunt to you, my friend." Mayhem drew a long, wicked blade from the sheath across his back and raised it toward the sky. "May you hear the death screams of our enemies wherever you might be."

His blood sang as he ran, the hunting instincts they all shared rising to the front of his mind. Everything else faded into the background. It was him, the enemy, and the hunt.

The scent trail led to a part of the forest he usually avoided. The shadows were deeper here, the moss thick enough to hide a loose rock or rotten log. He kept his eye out for the serpents that dwelled in this area. Some were harmless, but others were venomous, short-tempered creatures who lashed out at anything that disturbed them.

He slowed, scanning both the ground and the branches

overhead for potential hazards as he approached the landing site.

Judging by the damage to the forest, they'd come down hard and fast. The canopy was ripped open like a gaping wound. The stench of chemicals and char hung heavily in the air, making it impossible to scent the enemy, but they had to be here somewhere.

He spotted the ship first. It was smaller than he'd expected. Was it a scout ship? A recon drone?

Something moved on the other side of the clearing. He tensed, went still, and imagined himself to be one with the rocks and trees around him. His tawny fur wasn't quite the right color to be true camouflage, but it was enough to help him blend in.

As it turned out, he didn't have to worry about being seen. The enemy was too busy being assaulted by their own equipment to notice anything else. As he watched, a loud commotion erupted along with a flurry of sudden motion and then a large yellow *something* exploded into being. The sole occupant of the ship was hit from behind and went down hard. They didn't get up right away, and when they did, they struggled to their feet unsteadily. Once up, they turned to glare at the yellow thing like it had attacked them on purpose.

The whatever-it-was hissed and slowly deflated until it was little more than a sad, yellow patch of material that covered a few square meters of the forest floor.

The enemy was similar to Bysshe in basic body type. Were they human? Maybe. He'd only seen them on vids, but that species had crafted the android, so it was likely. What was a human doing out here?

He watched as they assessed the damage to their belongings. Not as tall as Bysshe, but not short, either. They were solidly built, unlike the verexi, and the clothing they wore was wet with something thick and unpleasant that made the fabric cling and bunch so he couldn't see their body well.

It didn't look like they were armed, though.

He stayed rooted in place, fascinated, as the human raised a hand to sweep back a fall of hair that glowed dark red, like the embers of a dying fire. The moment they touched their hair, though, they pulled away immediately, their features wrinkled with disgust.

Then the human sighed in annoyance. "Something here is going to try to eat me. I just know it."

That voice. It spoke a language his translator recognized, so he understood what she said. However, the way they spoke was different. The words were softer. The tone lighter. He'd only heard that type of voice on vids. This was a *female*.

He'd never seen one before. Not face to face. The only species he'd ever seen other than his own were the verexi, and they were asexual. The pleasure bots their captors had provided to the fa'rel once they reached maturity were functional but featureless things. Biologically compatible, but that was all.

This was a real female. Not on a screen but here. On his planet... in his territory.

The thought had barely formed when the female reacted to something behind her. She turned away from him and then went still.

She was blocking his view, making it impossible to see

what she was looking at. He moved to one side, and while he did that, she removed one of her shoes.

What the fuck was she doing? What was... ah.

He saw the serpent a second before she threw her footwear at it. Was that the only weapon she had? Surely not. The others the verexi had paid to put an end to them had all been well-armed, a fact the fa'rel had appreciated. Their weapons and gear had been added to the armory. So far, they hadn't been able to take one of the ships before the remaining invaders had fled back to the stars. One day, they'd manage it.

Mayhem's gaze slid to the battered wreckage of the small ship the female had arrived on. Not that ship, though. It was nothing but scrap metal and salvage now. The female couldn't leave. What kind of mercenary was she?

The serpent came toward him and he got a good look at it. Not one of the venomous ones. If it had been larger, he'd have killed and brought it back for dinner, but it was too small to bother with, and he needed to keep his attention on the female.

She was the only threat here.

"Something might eat me eventually," she called after the snake as she limped over to pick up her shoe, "but it won't be you."

Mayhem sidestepped the serpent and moved into the open. His blade was raised and his whole body sang with tension as he nodded to the female. "That creature has no fangs and was no threat to you. I do. Surrender now and I will make your end swift and merciful."

He'd made this offer twice before. Both times, the

enemy had responded with violence. He expected nothing else from this one, but she surprised him.

Instead of going on the offensive, she turned toward him, raised her hands, and laughed. "Did that thing bite me after all? It must have because something as pretty as you can't possibly exist outside the gates of paradise."

3

SHE HAD TO BE DEAD. That was the only explanation for the appearance of the most attractive male Bella had ever seen. He was pretty enough to be an angel, but with those horns and the hint of fang she could see peeking out from his upper jaw, he was probably a demon.

Bella snorted derisively. Who was she kidding? With the life she'd led, he was *definitely* a demon. And a tempting one, too... if she were a few decades younger.

Alien biology made it tricky to guess a person's age, but her gut told her he was a youngster in his prime. Even when she'd been at her peak, someone like him would have still been light-years out of her league.

Of course, that was all a moot point, given that he'd just threatened to kill her.

Focus. She needed to focus.

She stayed where she was, hands raised in what she hoped he understood was a signal of surrender. "I give up. Surrender. Whatever. I'm kinda hoping you don't kill me, though. Swift or otherwise. If I'd wanted to die, I could have stayed on the *Bountiful Harvest*. She's probably at the bottom of a smoking crater by now."

Big, gold, and grumpy snarled, one side of his mouth curling up to show more fang. He held a bladed weapon in one hand. It was long enough her brain wanted to call it a sword, but who the hells carried a sword these days?

In fact, his entire outfit was like something out of a historical vid. Straps of leather crisscrossed over his chest, and a kilt-like garment made up of thick, overlapping strips of dark leather hung from his hips to the midpoint of his tree-sized thighs.

"How many were aboard? Were other ships involved in this attack? What was the plan this time?" he demanded.

"Attack? No, no. I was a passenger on a matchmaking cruise. You know, one of those 'see the galaxy, find your soulmate,' type things. I'm not a soldier. Even if I wanted to fight, what military would want someone my age?"

"Matchmaking cruise?" His expression was one of utter bafflement. Not a surprise. The way he looked, he clearly didn't need any help finding romantic partners. In fact, he probably had a waiting list.

She racked her brain to try to come up with an explanation that didn't sound pathetic and quickly realized there wasn't one. "Single women pay to travel together and visit other worlds. At every stop we'd have a few days to meet and mingle with prospective males looking for mates. That's it. So, unless you're afraid of being invaded by a bunch of single women, you've got nothing to worry about."

He didn't look convinced. "Why are you here?"

"Honestly? I have no idea. One second, everything was fine, the next... *Boom.* Our ship's star-drive failed or exploded or something and we fell back into normal space. The next thing I knew, we were all told to abandon ship." She jerked with her thumb toward the banged up remains of her escape pod. "I'm alone. I don't know if any of the others made it. There were other passengers and a small crew."

Reality finally dawned on her, or more accurately, reality came crashing through the bubble of denial she was living in and shattered it. Her ship had crashed. Everyone else might be dead or injured. And unless someone managed to get off a distress call, no one knew she was here.

Her knees threatened to buckle, and she decided to sit down before she fell over. She took a careful step backward and then another, keeping her eyes on her *demon* the whole time.

"I need to sit down. I'm not armed. I just... they're gone. That hadn't sunk in until now."

Something that might have been concern flickered across the male's features. The black lines that marked his forehead from mid-brow to his hairline made it hard to be certain, but he didn't tell her to stop moving.

Good enough.

She went back to the same mossy rock she'd been on before and sat down with a sigh. "Thank you."

"For not killing you? I haven't yet, but I still might."

She barked with laughter and lowered her hands to her lap. "Sure thing. Until then, thanks for letting me sit down."

"You have no weapons? At all?" He was moving again, prowling around the crash site with a smooth, gliding motion that reminded her of old vids she'd seen about long-extinct hunting cats back from Earth. Everything he wore was rustic and looked handmade. The kilt, the sword, the spear she could see strapped to his back. No shirt, only a few leather cross-straps and a couple of bands of leather tied around his biceps, holding two daggers in place.

He had sections of hardened leather bound to his lower legs, too. Greaves? She had no idea where she'd read the word, but it felt like the right one. Whoever he was, he'd come here dressed for combat not conversation. Though at least he had a translator. Otherwise, they wouldn't be conversing at all.

"No weapons. No shelter either." She gestured to the punctured emergency shelter. "I do have some food and things. Hungry?"

She didn't have anything else to offer him. Whoever he'd come here expecting to find, she wasn't it. She couldn't give him answers, so she'd have to hope he was open to bribery.

"You hunted already?" He cocked his head to one side, his amber eyes narrowing. "I thought you said you had no weapons. Or did you throw your shoe at something else before I got here?"

Was that a note of humor she heard? She hoped so. "I never said anything about hunting. I was talking about rations. There should be some in that container over there. Shall I check?"

She knew his answer before she'd voiced the question. He didn't trust her enough to let her do anything of the sort.

"No. I will look. You stay where you are." He sheathed his blade and went over to the container, keeping one eye on her as he bent to unlock the top and sort through the contents.

With him distracted, Bella took the time to get a better look at him. His hair was dark at the roots but faded to a tawny blond by the time it reached his shoulders. The cut was shaggy and uneven, as if his barber had been into the booze between clients. Or maybe he'd done it himself. He had a short beard not much longer than the fur that covered the rest of his body. It was thick, but she could still make out the high cut of his cheekbones and the hard line of his jaw beneath. His eyes were incredible. They were slightly rounder than a human's would be with no visible whites. Only the deep amber color of the iris around a jet-black pupil, all of it marked with a line of pure black fur that would have made a make-up artist jealous.

While she admired the view, the big alien went through the supplies. Food packets, water canteens, a first-aid kit and more were pulled from the container. He briefly examined and sniffed each item and then dropped it onto the pile growing at his feet.

He took a little more care with the flare gun and what looked like a fire starter, but after that she didn't recognize much. It wasn't surprising she didn't know what half the stuff was. Most of her adult life had been spent as the kept woman of a dangerous and very wealthy man. What she knew about survival gear could be written on the back of a cocktail napkin and still have room for a game or two of hangman.

"This has many useful things," her demon announced as he lifted the last item out and held it in his hand. "This is a transponder. Yes? An emergency beacon?"

"It is. Once we activate it, someone will come looking for me."

"No." He threw it against a large rock with enough force to crack the casing. Before she could say anything, he had his spear in hand and used the butt end to smash the transponder repeatedly. In less than a minute it was nothing but scrap.

"That was my only way off this planet!" she yelled at him. Probably not the smartest thing to do, but dammit, he'd destroyed her best chance of rescue. Unless the escape pod had its own beacon...

She looked that way before she could stop herself, and demon-guy followed her gaze.

"The ship has a tracker too?"

"No. I mean. I don't know. It's an escape pod. I don't know how it works." Her words came out too rushed to be believable. She needed to get her shit together right the hells now, or she was going to end up dead out here. She took a swift breath, squared her shoulders, and got to her feet.

"Look. Can we start again? My name is Bella, and I'd be grateful if you stopped breaking my stuff."

He turned to face her, the dappled sunlight falling on his golden fur. "I'm Mayhem, and none of this is yours. You are in my territory. Everything here is *mine*."

"You're claiming everything because I happened to crash here? That's not how property law works. Possession is nine-tenths of the law." She may not know much about survival gear, but when it came to the law and its many loopholes, she was an expert. Felix had enjoyed telling her about his business dealings, both legal and otherwise, and after each visit she would research what he'd told her, adding to her understanding of how her world worked. It was a way to pass the time, and it gave them a shared interest. That interest had protected her for years, long after Felix had lost any interest in her body.

"Your laws don't apply here. This is our world, and this is my land." He smirked, the wicked little smile doing things to his mouth that should be illegal. "So, I am the one in possession of everything here. Hmm. Maybe your laws apply after all."

He spun the spear in one hand, letting it arc through the air in a full circle before stopping it by bringing the butt down on the mossy ground. "I'm also the only one with a weapon."

"If you take everything I have, I'll die. I need those supplies." She was fairly certain she was going to die out here regardless of what supplies she had, but she protested anyway.

Mayhem considered and then nodded to himself. "If you tell me how to deactivate the other beacon, I won't take everything."

"Boy, you really don't want anyone coming down here. Do you?" It was a shitty deal, but what choice did she have? If she refused, he could kill her and trash the pod himself.

"You don't, either. Anyone who came here would be working for the verexi, and they won't react well to your presence. This is a verexi prison planet. No one is supposed to come here, and no one is allowed to leave."

Well, *fuck*.

"You thought I was an attacker, though. So clearly some people are coming here."

Mayhem uttered a low, unhappy noise she realized was a growl before he spoke. "They aren't here to rescue us. They're trying to kill us. Sometimes, they succeed." He glanced up at the sky. "And once they realize there's been an incursion, they'll come looking for you and any other survivors."

Her stomach twisted into a tight knot and she had to force her words past a lump that had suddenly appeared in her throat. "But not to save us."

"No. They'll want to kill you, too."

"I'm not thrilled with that plan." She needed to barter with him, but since he'd laid claim to everything already, she didn't have much to offer in exchange for his help. Maybe if she handed over the stuff he'd agreed to give her if she showed him how to turn off the transponder in the pod...

"You need to show me how to disable the other signal. Now." The butt of his spear hit the ground to punctuate his words.

"I bet all the females just love it when you bark orders at them," she muttered and got to her feet. The gel had finally dried, and she brushed more chunks of it off herself and out of her hair as she trudged over to the pod and tried to work out where the beacon would be.

The bottom part had been filled with supplies. So she reasoned that the beacon and other electronics should be up at the top.

"I think it's up here." Thanks to the automatic thrusters, the pod had landed more or less upright. Bella was almost as tall as most human men, but she still couldn't reach the only panel with any markings on it. It was dented and scratched up too badly for her to read what it said, but that had to be what they were looking for.

She clambered onto a nearby stone to get a better look.

It wasn't the best idea. She'd barely gotten up there before her foot slipped and she lost her balance. She threw out her arms instinctively and braced for impact... only that's not what happened.

Instead of hard ground and harder stone, she was caught midair and pulled in tightly against a broad, furry chest as arms like iron locked around her. She should have been mortified or terrified. Probably both. Instead, all she felt was a sizzling rush of heat that wiped away everything else.

She wanted him. More than that, she *needed* him in ways she'd never experienced before. She forgot about the crash and the fate of the others. She couldn't even remember how she'd wound up in Mayhem's arms. All she knew was she didn't want to let go of him. If she did, she might never get to feel this way again.

She breathed in the musky scent of him, letting herself get lost in the silky caress of his fur against her skin and the hard lines of his body. Her pulse quickened and her body throbbed in time to the rapid beating of her heart. Heat poured through her, melting her mind and making her thighs sticky with a sudden rush of longing that was as physical as it was emotional.

If he'd taken her to the ground and fucked her then and there, she would have let him. Hells, she'd have welcomed him.

"Whoa." She tried to slam the brakes on her libido before it made the jump to lightspeed. It wasn't a complete success, but she did manage to tear her mouth from his. She shoved backward against the wall of muscle that was his

chest and managed to gain enough space to breathe...
barely.

Dazed, panting, and clinging to the last shreds of her
dignity, she tried to sound resolute when she pointed
toward the ground. "Thank you for catching me. But you
have to put me down now."

He smirked and shook his head. "No."

"What? Yes! Down. Now." She was reduced to
monosyllables now. Not a good sign. What little brain
power she'd managed to muster wasn't going to last long.

"No." He bowed his head until they were almost nose to
nose. "I've changed my mind. Everything here is mine.
Including you."

4

CATCHING HER HAD BEEN INSTINCTIVE. In that moment he'd acted as if she was part of his clan and not a potential enemy. Dropping his weapon went against everything he knew, but the moment he touched her, he knew he'd made the right choice.

She was not his enemy. She was simply *his*.

Desire heated his blood and hardened his cock as a heady rush of lust and need coursed through him, battering his senses. He craved her, but it was more than that. She *called* to him, body and soul.

He planted his feet and cradled her against his chest as he fought to control himself before he tumbled them both to the ground. If he did that, he'd take her right there.

The thought of doing that—burying himself deep in her body—had his balls tightening in anticipation. He wanted to know everything about her. Scent. Taste. The way her soft hands would feel on his body. Would she touch his horns? Use them to steady herself as he fucked her?

He needed to find out. But first, he had to clarify things

for his little female. She thought she could tell him what to do. She was wrong.

"No." He lowered his head so they were eye to eye. "I've changed my mind. Everything here is mine. Including you."

This close to her he couldn't ignore the chemical reek that clung to her skin, clothes, and hair. He caught a tantalizing whiff of her true scent beneath it, but it wasn't enough. He needed more. Soon.

"The hells I am! I'm not your possession." Her voice crackled with emotion, and it wasn't annoyance. It was deeper and darker than that. "No one owns me. Not anymore. I'll never live that way again."

The tone even more than her words stopped him. He recognized it even through the fog of lust clouding his mind. She was afraid of being controlled... possessed. That was something he understood.

He set her down on the ground without letting go. He kept one arm around her waist, holding her against him and letting the proof of his desire be known even through the straps of leather that covered him.

She gasped and looked up at him, her eyes glazed over with a need that mirrored his own. Her cheeks were flushed, her lips parted. "I am not yours."

He could hear the determination in her voice. The defiance echoed with old pains. He cupped her heated cheek in one hand, ignoring the streaks of dirt and grime on her skin. "You are mine, but it won't be the same as it was before. I wouldn't do that to you. I understand..."

"I doubt that."

He snarled at her, frustration shredding his control with sharp claws. "Don't doubt it. I have been imprisoned.

Beaten. Abused." The words felt like acid on his tongue. None of them ever spoke about the time before. What the verexi had done to them. The lifetime of pain and suffering that was all they'd known until this place.

"You? You're beautiful. Strong. Fierce. You're everything every male aspires to be. Who would dare abuse you?"

Her words were barbed and intended to sting, but to him they were a cool spring on a hot day. She thought he was beautiful? He was a failed lab experiment. But this female. This real, breathing, female didn't see him that way.

What little blood was left in his brain flowed southward, and his mind threatened to stop working completely. "The verexi did. And I will never let that happen again. Not to me or my clansmen."

"Clansmen?" He didn't understand why that was the word she latched on to.

"Yes. My brothers. We escaped together."

"Escaped?" He could see her mind working, putting together the pieces. "So you got away, but now you're trapped here. You and your brothers. No females?"

"We took over the ship that brought us here. They lied and said it was so we could be free. They had intended to kill us, but we fought back and now they keep us here and claim they are *protecting* us."

He gave in to the need to touch her. He moved slowly, slipping one hand beneath the fabric above her hip so he could touch her skin. Then, he remembered the rest of her question. "No females. We were created in a lab. The verexi wanted soldiers they could control so they could wage war on their enemies."

"No females. Ever?"

He moved his hand higher, following the indent at her hip to her ribs and then upward until her breast was beneath his palm.

"No females. Sometimes they would give us pleasure bots to use, but I've never seen a female before. Not until you."

"Well, shit." Bella's skin flushed again, starting from beneath the collar of her shirt and rising until she was pink to the tips of her ears. "You're a virgin... and I am so going to spend eternity touring the nine hells for what I want to do to you right now."

"I've already been to hell. I won't go back." He thrust a thigh between her legs, letting the leather fall away to reveal the head of his aching cock as he rubbed it along the inside of her thigh. "And I am not letting you go anywhere without me."

"That sounds a lot like ownership." To his delight, Bella reached up to grab one of his horns where it curled by his cheek. She used it to pull his head down closer and then looked him in the eye. "I do *not* belong to you."

"Wrong. But I am starting to think that showing you the error of your assumptions will be enjoyable... for both of us."

If she'd had fur, it would have been standing on end, and he had to fight back the urge to chuckle at her display of anger.

She pushed back on his horn, trying to put some distance between them, but he didn't allow it. She gave up and glared at him instead.

"Only I could crash on a planet with almost no one on it and immediately attract the most annoying, dominant, arrogant male in the hemisphere. Maybe they didn't cover this wherever you grew up, but females like to be courted. Flirted with. Complimented. And it should be with someone closer to your own age. I'm old enough to be your..." She scowled and waved a hand vaguely. "Something inappropriate. I'm also slimy and covered in suspension gel that smells like several small, furry creatures died in the tank and were left to rot there.

Her deep green eyes flashed in defiance and she shook her head hard enough to make her hair whip around her face. "This insane thing between us—whatever it is—will not be happening."

Fascination warred with desire. In the end, desire won. "It already happened," he told her. "And while I have no idea how to court a female, I do know how to pleasure one. The bots provided to us all had basic instructional programming."

Her eyes widened, but he continued before she could interrupt. He wasn't used to holding long conversations, and he wanted to get the words out before the feel of her soft, lush body against his made him forget what he wanted to say. "Instead of flirtation, I will care for you, protect you, and provide you with countless orgasms."

She stared at him in silence for several long seconds before speaking. "That still sounds like ownership. A gilded cage is still a prison, no matter how many orgasms are included in the package."

He barely heard her. She consumed all of his attention. Her skin was soft and enticing. This close, he could see the delicate lines around her eyes, the creases deepening as she scowled at him.

"Are you even listening to me?" she asked.

"No. I am admiring you." He touched a finger to her cheek and smoothed it gently over the lines at the corner of her eye. "These are pretty." His hand kept moving until his fingers found her hair. It was stiff and sticky, but he ignored that. Her coloring was different from what he'd first thought. He wrapped his fingers in her tresses, lifting it until he understood. The dark color of her hair was streaked with lines of pure white, like moonlight. "You have stripes."

Bella laughed. "That's one way to put it. When humans get older, our hair usually turns white or silver. And those *pretty* things around my eyes are called wrinkles. Most men think they're ugly because they're proof that the woman bearing them is past her prime." Her jaw tightened and her chin lifted. "Like I said before. I'm too old for you."

He didn't know much about humans or females, but he did know a challenge when he heard one. "You're wrong."

"I'm not. I'm too old to be gadding about an alien forest with a buff, barely dressed boy half my age." Her voice hardened. "The ship I was on was full of women like me. Single. Lonely... stupid. We paid a lot of money to get ferried around the systems so we could meet interested, eligible males. Now all that's left are the dregs. Women like me. Too old. Too plain looking. Too weak or too strong." She blinked. "And just like me, they'll be here, on this planet. Alone. Shit. I need to find them."

Mayhem's mind was still reeling from the bombshells she'd dropped, and it took him a few seconds to catch up. She'd said it was a matchmaking cruise, but he hadn't really understood what that mean. Now, he did.

"You were looking for a male? You paid someone to do

this for you?" He grinned. "You should have come here first. I am your male." He bent his head and brushed his lips against hers. It was the first time he'd done this, but the moment their mouths met, he knew it was the right thing to do.

Her lips parted, probably to protest, but he took advantage of the opening to slip his tongue into her mouth. She tasted sweet, like the sun-ripened fruits Bysshe gathered and then fermented into the heady liquor they drank during their gatherings. Bella was just as delicious and even more intoxicating.

Her body softened against his, and he felt her surrender even before she uttered a soft moan of need and rose up on her toes to kiss him back.

"You are mine, Bella. Let me prove it to you."

"Yes. No." She tried to shake her head and pull away, but he held her hair in his fist and used it to control her.

He snarled in frustration. "Stop fighting me."

"I need to find the other women. Help them. Warn them..."

Ah. She was worried about the others. "If they are in the little pods like yours, they have landed in the territories of my brothers. Don't worry. They'll be safe."

She snorted. "Yeah because I'm so safe right now."

His next words surprised them both. "You will always be safe with me."

"If that's so, maybe we should pause this conversation long enough to deactivate that emergency beacon. Otherwise keeping me safe is going to get complicated. Right?"

Fuck. The beacon. He'd forgotten about it. If Menace or

any the others could see him now, they'd laugh at him. Well, first they'd laugh and then one or all of them would kick his ass for getting sloppy. "Right."

He didn't want to let her go. He wanted to bend her over the nearest rock and fuck her until she stopped denying the truth. She was his, dammit, and that meant he needed to protect her. He sighed. The beacon was too big a threat to ignore.

"Do not move," he told her. Then he stole one last kiss before they untangled themselves. He saw a hint of regret in her eyes, and it pleased him. She was feeling the same thing he was... and soon they could indulge themselves. He'd figure out the rest later. Much, much later.

He used the point of his spear to pry open the panel Bella had pointed out. After that it was a simple matter of bashing it until the lights stopped strobing and nothing worked anymore.

It only took another minute to gather up the supplies and secure them inside the container again. That would do until he could come back with some of the others to salvage it all. Bysshe would want to see this, too. And he'd want to see Bella.

Mayhem growled. He wasn't ready for that. For now, he wanted to keep her to himself.

"We go now." He took her hand and tried to lead her away.

"Words. You're going to need to learn how to use more of them." She shot him an annoyed look that was utterly adorable.

He liked that she wasn't afraid of him. It was the first time in his life someone other than his clansman or Bysshe had seen him as person and not something to fear. "My words were fine. We're going. You. Me. That way." He pointed in the direction of home.

"And what's that way?" she asked, dropping her voice on the last two words in mimicry of him.

"Home." He ran a finger over her wrist, noting the way the gel clung to her skin. That could not be comfortable. "And a place to bathe."

Bella perked up. "Bathe? You should have led with that. I can't wait to get cleaned up. This stuff is nasty." She tweaked at the front of her shirt. "Damn, these are my only clothes. I hope this washes out."

"I hope it doesn't."

She rolled her eyes. "And then what would I wear?"

He set off for home. He wanted to see her there, by his fire, and in his bed, and if he had his way, she'd never wear anything unless his brothers were around. "Nothing."

5

BELLA COULDN'T THINK STRAIGHT. Hells, she could barely hold a thought for more than a few seconds before it'd be pushed aside again. Dark desires filled her mind as her body cried out for things she'd never wanted before. Carnal things. Lustful things. And she wanted to do them all with Mayhem.

Maybe she'd hit her head during the crash. Fuck, maybe she was dead, and this was some strange version of the afterlife. It had to be something like that because she should not be feeling this way. She shouldn't be aching to get naked and nasty with an alien she'd only just met, never mind one half her age.

Or maybe he only looks young. Alien lifespans and all that. He might be older than I am. The little voice at the back of her mind was feeding her a line of bullshit and she knew it. Mayhem didn't just look young. He *was* young. Brash. Confident. Virile. And stars help her, innocent.

He'd never seen a woman before today. His only experience had been with pleasure bots... and if she understood him correctly, he'd been raised in a lab. Innocent wasn't the right word for what he was, and she still wanted to grab him by the horns and do very dirty things to him... with him.

Her head filled with images so graphic she blushed and ducked her head before he could see her. Distracted, she stumbled over a root and fell sideways, bumping into Mayhem.

He looked down at her, frowning. "This is taking too long. You move too slow."

"I'm doing my best."

"My best is better." He stopped, turned, and scooped her into his arms before she could protest.

"Uh. What are you doing?" she asked. Not the sharpest comment, but her mind had melted to slag the moment she'd found herself back in his arms.

"Taking you home."

"We were already doing that. Put me back down and I'll walk."

He shook his head and gave her a wicked little smile that made his eyes crinkle and showed a hint of fang. "I already said you're too slow. We'll do this my way."

That was the only warning she got before he took off running.

She was too big for most men to even lift, never mind carry like this. Mayhem kept her close to his chest, strong arms holding her firmly as he raced through the forest, hurdling over fallen logs and bounding over rocks with ease.

She wrapped one hand around the leather straps that crossed his chest and held on. As much as she hated to admit it, she couldn't do anything else.

When she'd finally had enough money and means to live her own life, she'd made a promise to herself. No matter what came her way, she'd never let anyone control her again. Only this felt different. At least, that's what she wanted to believe. Whatever was happening to her, it was messing up her mind as well as her body. That worried her, but what other choice did she have? If she tried to go after the others on her own, she'd be dead before dawn. Hells, she didn't even know where to start looking. Making her own decisions was important to her, but she wasn't going to die just because the only choices she could make were bad ones.

Bella buried her face against the warm, sleek fur of Mayhem's shoulder and closed her eyes. She was out of options... for now.

She couldn't tell how long he ran like that, but when he slowed, his breathing was barely elevated. He was in his prime. Strong, fit, and with speed and endurance to spare. If he wasn't trapped here, he'd have his pick of willing females.

Guilt and jealousy hit her with a double punch. Guilt because he only wanted her because he didn't have any other options, and jealousy because despite knowing this was wrong, she didn't want him to be with anyone else. She wanted him to want *her*. Which only proved that she wasn't in her right mind. Not even close.

He interrupted her inner monologue before it got anymore judgmental. "Welcome home, my falling star."

She opened her eyes. They were on the bank of a river, wide enough that the canopy of trees above didn't quite meet. Sunlight poured down through the gap, dancing on the water as it swirled around massive stones, some almost as big as her escape pod. On the far side of the river was a clear space around the trunk of a huge tree. She'd never seen anything like it. It was like a pillar of living wood that dwarfed everything else in the clearing. A fire pit, several small lean-tos, and... she squinted, trying to make out the details despite the distance. Stairs?

"Why does the tree of have steps built along the side?" she asked, not really aware she'd spoken aloud.

Mayhem chuffed with laughter and then set her down so he could point, guiding her gaze upward. "That's why."

Holy hells. High in the branches of the massive tree was a building. No, it was a house. With decks and railings and a roof and walls. The windows had shutters but no glass that she could see. The structure wasn't uniform because it had to accommodate the thick branches that rose up around and through the space, but it was definitely a house.

"You live in a treehouse?"

"We do. They're easier to defend and they don't flood in the rainy season. Most predators big enough to bother us can't climb that high." He shrugged. "It works."

Bella decided to ignore the fact he'd said *we*, as if it was a forgone conclusion this was her home now. "It looks nice." Her mind threw in some more descriptors she didn't say aloud. Rustic. Drafty. Leaky. Primitive. Not to mention really damned high.

"It is home." Mayhem bowed his head to nuzzle at her neck. "I'll show it to you soon. But first, I promised you a bath."

He caught her hand and walked up the bank. Shit. Was he going to toss her in the river? The water looked deep, and it flowed fast enough she doubted she'd be able to keep her footing. "Uh. That's not a bath. That's a river."

"There's a natural pool nearby. The water is quieter and the sun warms it to a nice temperature."

She eyed him dubiously and dragged her feet. "I bet it's got leeches, or snakes, or something with big teeth that's going to try to eat me."

He turned back to her and his amber eyes almost glowed with raw desire. "The only thing that will eat you is me, and you will enjoy every second of it."

Fucking hells. For an innocent, Mayhem possessed a shockingly dirty mouth... and she liked it. She tried and failed to suppress the shiver of anticipation that ran through her, need making her clit throb and her pussy slick with fresh proof of her need.

Mayhem grinned and inhaled deeply, making no pretense about what he was doing. "You smell delicious when your need rises. I want to know what you taste like.

Another shiver raced through her. "Where did you even learn about that sort of thing? I thought you'd never seen a woman before."

"Not in real life, no. Our captors let us view all sorts of vids, though. Once we got old enough, it was easier to give us vids and pleasure bots to spend our energy on than to try and control us another way." His face darkened. "Bysshe said it was one of the few times the scrawnies used the carrot instead of the stick."

They made their way up the river for a few minutes in silence while Bella considered what he'd told her. If being given porn and access to pleasure bots was considered a kindness, his life must have been a harsh one. Who'd done this to him, and how had he wound up here?

"Scrawnies. You mean the verexi?" she asked. He'd mentioned this was a verexi planet. Had they been the ones to create him?

"Yes. You know of them?"

"I do." She'd never met one. Not many had, but she'd seen them in photos and vids. They were physically fragile and didn't cope well with space travel, which was ironic given their territory contained some of the richest deposits of Talium-6 ever discovered. It was the most valuable substance in the universe, with a handful of crystals able to power a star ship's hyperdrive for years.

The verexi used AI-piloted ships and remotely powered drones to transport the Talium-6 to their buyers and stayed close to their home planet, the one place the laws of the Galactic Legion allowed them to weaponize space vessels operated by an AI.

"The verexi *made* you? Why?"

"Because they hate being seen as weak." Mayhem's voice was harsh. "They tried to create a race of enslaved soldiers to fight for them. They made us instead. We are fighters, but we'll never be slaves. We're too defiant. Too strong-willed. Our captors were about to end the project and kill us, but something changed at the last minute. We never learned why."

He shrugged and helped her over a slick, mossy rock too big for her make it over on her own. "They brought us here instead. Promised us freedom, support, and supplies. It was all lies. They meant to kill us here. Maybe to hide the evidence? Bysshe was our only source of information, and by then the scrawnies suspected he was helping us."

She nodded. "So they stopped telling him what was going on."

"Yes. They were right about him, but by then it was too late. He warned us about the plan to kill us. We rebelled and crashed the ship. Now we're prisoners here."

Even in her current state, Bella understood. "You're still trapped, but in a bigger cage."

He growled. "They think it's a cage. We know better. It's our *world*, and we will defend it and ourselves."

He turned to face her and then pulled her into his arms. "I will defend you, too. You are mine, falling star. You are safe with me."

Safe was not the word she'd use to describe Mayhem, but before she could argue, he lifted her off her feet and carried her past a thick grove of trees into paradise.

The pool he'd promised was there, so crystal clear she could see down to the bottom. It was gravel and smooth stones, with not a fish or creepy-crawly thing to be seen. Even better, the water didn't look that deep, which was good because she'd never learned to swim. This, though... this she could handle.

The far end of the pool had a small waterfall only a meter or so high, fed by a tributary stream. The dappled shadows shifted as a breeze stirred the leaves and foliage, and the air was filled with the musical sounds of flowing water, the breeze in the trees, and the occasional trill of what she guessed was an avian of some kind. Though for all she knew it might be anything. This was a strange planet, after all.

Until this cruise, she'd never left her homeworld. Tova was one of the last major human colonies in existence, but it wasn't much to look at. The planet was only partially terraformed, and the population was mired in poverty and corruption. Humanity had reached for the stars, imagining a future of expansion and abundance. They'd found the Galactic Legion instead. Older races with far more power and knowledge had already laid claim to the stars, and they didn't want to share.

Mayhem carried her to the edge of the water before setting her down on a relatively level patch of ground. He palmed her ass as he released her and then moved a few steps away and started undressing.

"What are you doing?" she asked. It was a stupid question, but it was out of her mouth before she could stop it.

"Leather doesn't like being soaked in water. So, I'm taking it off."

"Uh. But you're a cat." *Fuck*, her brain and her mouth had disconnected, leading to total filter failure. "I mean, you look like a feline—an Earth species—and uh, they don't like the water. I thought I'd be doing this alone."

He set his weapons down on a nearby rock with meticulous care and then straightened, his hands working on something near his waist. A moment later the leather kilt fell to the ground. "You were wrong."

She almost bolted. Seeing him naked and hungry triggered a primal part of her brain. He was a predator, and the way he looked at her made it clear she was his prey. If she ran, he'd chase her. She'd never have the chance to get away from him, and if she was being honest, she didn't want it. The way he looked at her was intoxicating.

She deliberately turned her back to him and walked into the clear water of the pool. A few steps into the water she kicked off her shoes and left them to soak. Stars knew they needed it. The water was cool compared to the warm air but not cold. She kept walking.

"You're still dressed," Mayhem pointed out, his words heavy with amusement and what she thought might be a hint of frustration.

"I'm multitasking. My clothes need cleaning as much as the rest of me." She kept walking until the water reached her hips. Confident that she could stand if needed, she let herself sink down until the water closed over her head. She scrubbed at her face and hair until the last traces of gel were gone.

She broke the surface and spun around as a low growl came from behind her. Momentary panic faded as she realized it was Mayhem.

"First lesson in surviving here is this. Never turn your back on what's hunting you," he rumbled as his arms snaked around her, hauling her against his hard, very naked body.

"You're a predator, but you're not going to hurt me. If you wanted to do that, you would have done it already."

"You're right." His hands moved over her body so gently she didn't realize what he was doing until it was too late. Bits of cream fabric rose to the surface. He'd shredded her top.

"Hey! No hurting my clothes, either," she yelped and tried to gather up the tattered remains of what had been her shirt and pants.

"You turned your back on me. Now I've caught you, and I'm going to show you why you shouldn't do that."

"You already admitted you aren't going to hurt me." She gave up trying to cover herself and turned in his arms so she could see his face. He looked like a wild animal from Earth's distant past—wild, handsome, and fierce.

"There are other kinds of punishment. I've read about them. Pain is only one path." His next words were accompanied by a languid purr. "There's also pleasure. So much of it you will beg me to stop, and when I do, you'll beg me to start again."

His mouth sealed hers, cutting off anything she might have said. It was probably a good thing because the only words in her head right then were a resounding *oh, hells yes*.

She was in serious trouble.

6

IT WASN'T JUST DESIRE FOGGING his mind and turning his cock to stone. It was the realization that this beautiful female wasn't afraid of him. He'd seen the way her muscles tensed and her eyes widened as he'd stripped off his gear. She recognized what he was, and she'd turned her back on him anyway. She was maddeningly defiant and recklessly brave. She had no weapons, no claws, or fangs he'd seen. She had no defenses either, no protective armor, no horns to shield her head, and her skin was as soft as a flower petal.

Unless... the thought rose from the back of his mind like a dark shadow. What if she was manipulating him with her body? He craved her to the point of madness. Even now he was caressing her, washing her clean so he could taste her skin and memorize what she tasted like. He needed her. Wanted to protect her. Was this how humans survived? It didn't seem likely. Not when she'd fought so hard not to give in...

And the truth was, right now he didn't care if it was a trick or not.

His mouth mated with hers, their tongues twining, though he didn't recall when she opened her mouth to him. Their kisses were deeper now, bodies skin to fur, her soft hands buried in his hair, pulling him closer.

Fuck yes. This was better than any experience he'd had with the pleasure bots. That had been empty fucking. This was something else.

"Mine." The word rose from his throat, accompanied by a deep-throated rumble usually brought on by his own hand or the brief release the bots could offer. It had never happened before release, though. Not until he'd found her. If she could draw this sound from him with nothing more than a touch, he was never letting her go.

Bella tugged at his hair until he raised his head to look at her. "No. I can't do that. No promises. No possession. Just us. Here and now. Don't say anything else. Okay? The risk of regret is high enough already."

Regret? The word stung him. "You expect to regret this? Why?"

He didn't wait for her to answer. Instead, he strode through the water, carrying her to a spot he knew—a large, smooth, sun-warmed boulder on the far side of the pool.

She didn't speak until he'd set her down again, staying quiet even as he positioned them so she sat upright, her legs wrapped lightly around his torso and her hands on his shoulders.

"I'm not worried about me," she said softly.

"Explain. Quickly." He continued to touch her as they spoke. He needed to. He craved the feel of her under his hands, the soft press of her body against his.

"You're..." She raised a hand to make a sweeping gesture

that encompassed most of his body. "Amazing. And since I can't seem to stop myself from wanting you in every way imaginable, I've decided to give in to the madness. But once we snap out of this, it would be best if you haven't committed yourself to anything." She touched his face and smiled, but he saw something bittersweet in her expression. "Enjoy the moment, Mayhem. Don't worry about the future."

He'd lived his life that way, seizing on the small moments because none of them believed they had much of a future. But that had been before they'd broken free. Since then, he'd built a home and the beginnings of a life.

"No." He caught her by the hips and pulled her against him, letting his cock press against the seam of her pussy. "Mine. Always."

"No," she said, the word firm but quiet.

She didn't believe him. Stubborn female. He'd have to prove it to her.

"Yes." He reached between them, cupping the soft mound of her breast in his hand. She moaned, betraying her need. The tip of her breast hardened, and he lowered his fingers to touch her there.

The next moan was louder.

Curious, he kissed his way down the column of her neck, not stopping until his lips found her nipple. He sucked on it, drawing it into his mouth, and she shivered. Her fingers tightened on his hair. Her pussy creamed and he bucked his hips, grinding against the enticing wet heat.

It would be so easy to slide into her, claim her, fuck her until they both saw stars, but first...

He moved lower, nuzzling the soft pillow of her

stomach, and then went lower still. The scent of her need perfumed the air and he gave in to the desire to taste her. He caught her legs in his hands, pulling them from around his waist to raise them higher. She tipped backward, letting go of him to steady herself. Perfect.

"Lie back."

"You don't need…"

"Hush. The only sounds I want to hear from you are cries of pleasure. Now. Lie. Down."

She scowled and stuck out her tongue before lying back on the flat rock. Her submission poured rocket fuel on the fire already raging inside him, and then he dove into the flames and let them burn.

Sweet. Hot. Perfect. Her taste exploded on his tongue. He understood what to do on principle, but learning what made his female quiver and moan was almost as pleasurable for him as it was for her. He licked and suckled, discovering what she liked best. Her responses inflamed him, and when she gasped and caught hold of his horn to pull him closer, he began making that low, deep rumbling noise again. The sound rolled through him, vibrating against her clit, and Bella began to writhe in pleasure.

"Oh fuck. Yes. Don't stop. Please don't stop. That is…" Her words trailed off into wordless moan.

He had no intention of stopping. This was something he'd never expected to experience. A willing and eager female, beautiful and unafraid.

He latched on to the tender nub of her clit and sucked hard enough that she cried out again, arching her hips off the rock to grind her sex against his mouth. "More. Use your fingers. Please, Mayhem."

Please. The word resonated deep in his soul. No one had ever said that to him before. He gave her what she asked for, making sure his claws were fully retracted before sliding a finger into her sweet pussy, not stopping until he was deep inside. Her inner walls flexed and gripped him, the tight heat so tempting he nearly withdrew to replace his fingers with his dick.

He didn't. Not yet. Her passage was too tight, and he didn't want to hurt her. Instead, he slid another finger inside, flexing them, stretching her gently while giving her nothing but pleasure.

Her release was glorious, building to a peak that left her mindless and wild. Her moans and cries filled the air, the scent of her wrapping around his senses as she arched and trembled beneath him. He had done this to her. Made her boneless with pleasure.

Her legs slipped from his shoulders, and she uttered a soft, breathy moan that filled him with pride. He looked down at her for a moment, drinking in the sight of her.

He stroked his hand down her body, from the valley between her breasts and down

toward her pussy. "So beautiful."

"You only think that because I'm the only woman you've ever seen."

She was arguing with him again. He liked it, but now wasn't the time it. "I've seen many on vids. I still think you are beautiful, and I will prove it to you eventually, but not now. It's not time for talking."

Her brows lifted and a hint of a smile curved one corner of her mouth. "What time is it, then?"

"Time for lesson number two." He caught her by the

hips and pulled her in tightly against his groin. "You cannot survive here alone. I will protect you. In exchange, you will give me what I want."

She bit back a moan and gave a tiny nod.

"And if I say no?"

"You won't." He shifted his hips back, guiding his cock to her entrance and pressing far enough inside to make his point.

"I might."

"No. You won't. Because you want this as much as I do."

He forced himself to hold still, waiting for her to give him what he really wanted... her surrender.

He didn't have to wait long.

7

Bella threw her last reservations and doubts into a box and tossed them to the proverbial curb. Fuck it. She was alone on a dangerous planet, surrounded by things that wanted to kill her... and one sexy as hells alien who wanted something else. He wanted her.

It was not a difficult decision. "Yes."

She braced herself, expecting him to power into her and take what he so clearly wanted. He didn't.

Mayhem moved slowly, easing himself into her and giving her body time to adjust to him. There was a whole lot of him to get used to, including something that felt like... ridges. Stars and fucking novas, she could feel each one slide past her opening to caress parts of her she'd never known existed.

He kept moving until he filled her completely, their bodies merging as his eyes bored into hers. He took her hand in his and tugged, guiding her into a sitting position and placing her hand on his shoulder.

Then he cupped her face in his hand and leaned it to kiss her. "Say it again."

Something warm and wonderful bubbled up inside her, and her answer was accompanied by a soft ripple of laughter. "Yes. I'll give you what you want."

She tightened her inner walls around his cock. "Because you asked so nicely."

He growled something she couldn't quite hear and pulled back slowly, not stopping until he was almost fully withdrawn. "I didn't ask."

He surged into her, his cock plunging into her pussy and his tongue diving into her mouth at the same time.

She forgot how to breathe, how to think. All she could do was cling to him as he took what she offered and gave her back more than she'd ever imagined possible. She sank her fingers into the fur of his shoulder, her legs looped lightly around his hips.

His kisses were hard, demanding, and so full of heat it was almost like being branded. Her lungs were burning by the time she remembered to breathe again. She sucked in a lungful of air, her heart pounding like a hammer against her ribs. He might be a demon after all... and if he was, she was ready to sign her soul away if she got more of him in trade.

Water slapped against the rock as he took her, every stroke sending cool water splashing against the bottom of her thighs. The contrast in temperatures added new depths to her pleasure. She lost herself to it, her need building, her body reaching for something just out of reach.

She caught his lower lip between her teeth and nipped him. His response was to speed up, that tiny bit of pain spurring him on.

She did it again. This time, he made a sound somewhere between a growl and a groan. He shuddered beneath her touch, and she knew his control hung by a thread.

She curled her nails into his shoulder and tightened her body around his cock.

He drove into her one more time and came with a roar.

She relaxed and enjoyed the show. She'd already come once. It wasn't possible to come again so soon. At least, that's what she thought.

Mayhem threw back his head and roared again, his cock changing and thickening until she could feel his ridges flare and pulse. They were locked together like that, and the sensation sent her tumbling into another orgasm even stronger than her first.

Time stretched out like taffy, prolonging every moment of bliss. She wanted to stay there forever, but reality gradually returned.

The murmur of the river, the sun-warmed stone hard beneath her back, the slow throb of Mayhem's cock still inside her, and a faint tingling sensation around her wrists.

She pulled her hands away from Mayhem and stared at them, looking for what had caused the feeling.

"What in the nine hells?" She scrubbed one hand over the back of the other wrist. She had marks there, dark lines in her skin.

At the same time, Mayhem stiffened and snarled. His hand slapped his chest like he was trying to swat a fly, but she didn't see anything. Not at first. Then, as she watched, dark lines appeared on his chest. Three parallel marks started at each shoulder and crossed his chest to intersect in the center and continue down to his ribs.

"What just happened?" she asked.

Mayhem gave her a smug, satisfied grin. "I made you scream again."

She rolled her eyes at him. "Believe me, I haven't forgotten that. I meant this." She held up her wrists and then pointed to his chest.

He shook his head. "I don't know. It burned for a moment and then..." He took her hand, turning it over so he could trace the pattern over her skin. His touch sent little shivers up her arm, like the skin was more sensitive now.

"You look good with stripes."

"So do you, handsome. But what do they *mean*?"

He pressed her hand to the center of his chest, so her marks touched his. They were almost identical, save for the fact hers were smaller. He moved his free hand to his shoulder and flexed his fingers. Claws appeared, and he drew them carefully across the marks on his chest. They lined up perfectly.

"So we have identical markings now?"

"We do. We match." He withdrew from her gently and then pulled her off the rock and into his arms. "We are one."

"No. Nope. Nuh-uh," she protested. "It can't be that simple. If all it took to find a soulmate were matching tattoos, there wouldn't be a single human left in the galaxy."

Mayhem ignored her. Typical. Men always did that when you said something they didn't want to hear. She was about to repeat herself, but she barely got a word out before she was blinded by a flash of brilliant light.

"What was that?"

The answer came a few seconds later as a crash of thunder rolled across the sky.

"We're going inside. This is no place to be during a storm."

She didn't argue. She'd only seen a few storms in her life, but even she knew the dangers of being out in the open during weather like this. She nodded and buried her face against his chest as he carried her to the far shore. He set her down beside a moss-covered root and pointed to it. "Sit there. Do not move until I come back."

"Quit barking orders at me," she grumbled.

He pointed to the root and flashed his fangs at her. "Sit!"

She sat, but she didn't stop talking. "I'm not a child. For fuck's sake I'm old enough to be your mother, so don't take that tone of voice with me again."

Mayhem was already on the move, and after a few more choice turns of phrase, she stopped talking and watched. He didn't wade through the pool again. Instead, he crossed further down, where the river was narrower but the water moved much faster. He leaped from rock to rock with the speed and grace of a predator, once again reminding her that whatever he was, Mayhem wasn't even close to being human.

He gathered up his weapons and gear and even remembered to pick up her shoes. Would she still be considered naked if she had shoes on? Once they got inside, she'd have to figure out something, because mister "we match" had shredded the rest of her clothing.

The sky darkened and everything fell into gloomy shadows. The air was close and humid, and the forest had gone eerily still. Bella wrapped her arms around herself despite the heat, warding off a chill that had nothing to do with the weather. It wasn't safe out here.

She briefly considered heading for the structure Mayhem had pointed out earlier but decided against it. Bossy or not, he knew this place far better than she did. If he wanted her to stay put, he probably had a good reason.

He was on his way back to her when the storm finished its warmup and moved on to the main act. Lightning streaked from the sky, thunder boomed, and her world exploded into light and noise.

She tried not to jump out of her skin and kept her eyes glued to Mayhem. He'd made it halfway across the river now. She watched him bound from stone to stone as the lightning streaked across the sky, so bright the after images partially blinded her. He was almost lost in the gloom, but she caught the moment a massive thunderclap shattered the air. The sudden noise made him start and he nearly fell, but instead of stopping to regain his balance, he bounded to the next rock, somehow reorienting himself in midair. In that moment he looked more animal than man, and Bella was reminded again that whatever Mayhem was... he wasn't human.

He made one final, massive leap to reach the shore, giving her a cocky grin as he closed the distance between them.

The rain started a few seconds later. He ran to her, head down and shoulders hunched against the weather. It was too loud to talk, but when he offered her his hand, she understood what he wanted. She took it, rising to her feet to let him pick her up yet again. She'd never been carried so much in her life, and part of her was starting to enjoy it.

He brought her to the clearing. It was the one she'd seen earlier with temporary structures and a fire pit ringed and lined with river rock. What little she could see with the lashing rain and wind looked simple and rustic, but it was shelter, and that's more than she'd have if Mayhem hadn't found her.

She'd never experienced true poverty, though she'd seen it often enough. She'd been one of the lucky ones. Her father had kept her fed, sheltered, and educated until his health failed. Then he'd found her a new benefactor, Felix. She'd gone with him because she was smart enough to know that opportunities were hard to come by. As young as she was, she'd been too practical to hold on to her girlish hopes and dreams.

Going on this matchmaking cruise had been her way of trying to find the things she'd never had... like love. Instead, she wound up here with Mayhem, and whatever this thing was between them, it wasn't love. She probably didn't deserve that kind of happiness, not after the life she'd led. And Mayhem deserved so much better.

But right now, neither of them had much choice, so she pushed her regrets aside and focused on the present. Mayhem would protect her, and that protection came at a price she was more than happy to pay. He'd brought her more pleasure in one afternoon than she'd believed possible, and the day wasn't over yet. She had to be practical.

Even as she thought it, her eyes dropped to the marks on her wrists and a tiny voice whispered that if this wasn't love, that didn't mean it wasn't a good thing. Maybe it was something even better.

She ignored everything it said. That little voice was never right about *anything*.

Mayhem guided her to the stairs that led up to the treehouse. The treads were solid planks of wood that looked safe enough, but where she expected to see risers filling in the back of each stair was nothing but empty air. The stairs spiraled up the trunk, each plank anchored to the main tree on the inner curve. The outer curve was left open, without a railing or even a rope to grasp.

She looked back at Mayhem and then pointed up the stairs. "You're clearly not afraid of heights."

He tilted his head quizzically. "Why would I be?"

She chuckled. "Of course you aren't. Someone who can race through a forest without breaking a sweat and leap across rivers without getting their feet wet wouldn't be concerned about a little elevation."

She faced forward, placed one hand against the trunk of the tree, and started up the stairs. "I can't do any of that. So I'm trusting you to stop me from falling to my death if I slip."

Mayhem placed a steadying hand at the small of her back. "You will not fall."

She believed him.

One advantage to their current position quickly became obvious. The structure above them shielded her from the worst of the weather. The rain couldn't reach them, though an occasional blast of wind would be strong enough to make her stop and lean against the tree until she felt steady again. Mayhem didn't rush her. He was a calm, constant presence behind her, his hand resting lightly on her back.

She kept her head up and her eyes forward. *Keep going,*

she told herself. It was the motto of her life so far, though it had never quite been this literal.

They reached the top structure and she found herself on a solid deck built to accommodate the thick branches of the tree that continued to grow far up into the canopy. A quick glance back told her they were an alarming distance above the ground, and she made a mental note not to look down again unless it was absolutely necessary. To her relief, she noted that the deck had a railing running around it, though it was lower than she would've liked.

Mayhem guided her toward the largest of several structures that sprawled across a surprisingly expansive area. She quickly revised her earlier assessment. This wasn't a simple treehouse. It was an entire complex.

The moment she crossed the threshold, the noise of the storm faded. The wind and rain couldn't reach her here, and that awareness soothed away some of the tension she carried. Not all of it, but some.

Feeling more at ease, Bella took her first look at Mayhem's home. It was not what she expected. The structure was as basic as she'd assumed from the outside. The walls were made of planed boards, rough looking but relatively even. More boards were set into the walls to act as shelving. Some held easily identified items like dishware and cooking utensils. Others were laden with what looked like mechanical and electronic parts that seemed entirely out of place.

Why did he have those? What possible use could he have for electronics in a well-built but still primitive treehouse?

Her curiosity drew her further inside. The gentle sound

of rain on the roof attracted her attention and she glanced up at the roof. Wide support beams created a framework for what looked like slabs of metal. She narrowed her eyes and stopped moving to get a better look. It was definitely metal. In fact, it looked like it was part of the ship, or had been at some point. Something about that pinged an alarm at the back of her mind, and it took her only a few seconds to register what the problem was.

"Holy hells, Mayhem! Why are we sheltering from the storm under a metal roof? Are you trying to fry us?"

He actually looked offended for a second. "I'm not stupid, and I have better survival instincts than that. Lightning rods are positioned around my home."

Well, that was a surprise. "You have lightning rods?"

"We do." His shoulders straightened, and she could almost swear he puffed out his chest with pride. "We made them ourselves once the first storm had passed. We only had the wreckage of our ship as shelter back then, and the hull attracted far too many lightning strikes.

He glanced up at the roof. "It still does, but it's the most durable building material we have. The verexi were supposed to send supplies for us, but since they planned on killing us, most of what they sent were empty containers or out-of-date supplies and materials."

The story was both horrifying and familiar. Every species and governing body seemed to have at least a few things in common. They all had their share of corruption, they all had a dubious relationship to the truth, and none of them spent currency unless they had to. "So you've made do with what you had on hand. Needs must and all that."

Mayhem nodded but hung back, clearly giving her the

opportunity to look around and admire his home. It was simple but comfortable. Surprisingly comfortable in fact. While much of the furniture was handcrafted from the same yellowish wood as the walls and stairs, some of the contents had clearly come from somewhere else. A large bench had a back that looked upholstered with matching cushions fitted over the wood of the seat.

While she was busy exploring, Mayhem closed the main door and then moved around the room, drawing the shutters closed on every window until the room was almost dark and the noise of the storm was muffled enough she barely heard it. She could still hear the patter of rain on the roof, but considering how fierce the storm was, something must be laid over the metal to dampen the noise.

She expected him to light a candle or a lantern of some kind, but instead he reached out to a small panel fastened to the wall. She heard a click, and then the entire place filled with soft, buttery light.

In the gloom she hadn't noticed the glow-pods hanging from the beams, but now she could see them clearly.

"You have power? Here?"

He chuffed with smug laughter. "I have power. Heat. Running water... of a sort." He touched one of the walls and then fixed her with a look that made her mind melt a little around the edges. "Welcome home, Bella. What I built is now yours to enjoy."

She took one last look around and then walked over to Mayhem and tucked her hand into his larger one. Maybe that crazy little voice was right... maybe.

8

MAYHEM HADN'T EXPECTED the sense of pride he felt as he showed Bella around his home. He didn't know what sort of home she'd had before landing here, but it had been impossible to miss her apprehension at what she'd find inside. That irked him a little. He wasn't an animal, despite what the verexi believed. The scrawnies had named them fa'rel, which was an old word meaning a wild beast.

The verexi were wrong. He was a thinking, feeling male. Not an animal.

"We found an entire crate of these with the supplies they left for us. They were all broken, but we managed to repair enough of them to ensure we all have one." He gestured to the heating cubc that took up one corner of the small kitchen. It was large enough to warm the entire room, and the upper surface doubled as a cooktop. Bysshe had taught them to boil their water and cook their food to avoid getting sick. He'd been dubious at first but had quickly learned to like his meat cooked. It was far better than the shapeless dollops of ground raw meat the verexi had fed them.

"Running water, as promised," he said as she followed him into another room. The glow-pods here were set into the wall and could be activated by a touch. Bella watched him turn on the first one and then activated the last two herself. Good. He wanted her to feel at home here.

"How?" she asked as she looked around at the bathtub, shower area, and toilet.

He pointed upward. "Several cisterns up there gather rainwater. The pipes are salvaged from the ship. The wastewater is carried away by more pipes and gravity. The fixtures were in the supplies the scrawnies sent. It really was the strangest assortment of stuff."

Bella wrinkled her nose. "They probably offloaded whatever junk they could find to stuff in the containers. I mean, do verexi even take baths? You'd think they'd be afraid to slip on the soap and break every bone in their spindly bodies."

He burst out laughing. "We can only hope they all die that way." Then he drew her into his arms, his cock stirring at the thought of the two of them together in the tub. "You will never have to worry about that, though. I will hold you while you bathe, so there is no risk of falling."

Bella lifted her head slightly to look him in the eye. "You did a pretty good job of holding on to me when we were in the pool today. Speaking of which... why did we use the pool when you have indoor plumbing?"

A twinkle in the depths of her deep green eyes told him she had already guessed the reason, but he answered her anyway. "Because it was faster that way. I knew how much you wanted to get clean."

"Oh yes, of course. That was entirely for my benefit." She smiled and touched the center of his chest where the marks intersected. A pleasant tingle spread outward from there, quickly becoming a fire that threatened to burn him to ash where he stood.

He bowed his head to kiss her. The full curves of her ass filled his hands as he pulled her in tightly to his body. "It was very beneficial... for both of us." He nipped her lower lip. "Next time will be better."

"Next time. As in now? But we just..." he cut off whatever else she was about to say with another kiss. She had to feel the hard line of his cock pressed against her soft stomach. Didn't she understand what that meant? He wanted her again, and he would have her.

"Next time will be in my bed." He grinned down at her once the kiss ended. "Maybe two times. Then I think we'll want to shower. The water isn't heated, though, so I will stay with you to keep you warm."

"Uh huh." He heard the buzz of amusement in her voice. "And that will also be entirely for my benefit?"

"No. That will benefit us *both*. I never had anything of my own before I came here. Now I have a home. Privacy. Freedom." He squeezed her ass with both hands and bowed his head to graze his fangs along the side of her throat. "And a female to share it with."

She shivered and closed her eyes as her head tipped to the side, baring her neck in submission. *Fuck yes*. She might not understand what she was offering, but it didn't matter.

Part of her was ready to accept what he already knew. She belonged to him.

It wouldn't be long before she was his in every way he could imagine. He'd prove it to her one orgasm at a time.

Dark had set in before he let her out of bed again, and that was only because they were both famished. He cooked two steaks while Bella watched from her seat near the window. She'd opened the door and windows again, and a gentle breeze blew through the rooms.

To his amusement, Bella had donned his leather kilt. It was far too big for her, but she'd draped it over one shoulder so the belt fell diagonally across her body and the leather straps covered most of her central torso. The straps moved when she did, providing tantalizing glimpses of her body that vanished as quickly as they appeared.

"The verexi could have at least sent along some clothes or blankets or something. Did they expect you all to go naked?" she asked.

"We weren't given clothes. I assume they'd have given us armor if we'd turned out to be the fighters they'd intended us to be, but we weren't."

"No clothes. Ever?" Bella sounded horrified. He didn't understand her reaction. The verexi wore light fabrics wrapped in intricate patterns around their bodies, but the cloth was almost translucent and didn't do anything to hide their bodies. They'd watched countless hours of entertainment vids, and he knew that clothing varied wildly from species to species. Some wore layers of garments while some wore little or nothing. Then he remembered that the few humans he'd seen on those programs were usually dressed.

"I assume they didn't think it was necessary. We do have fur."

Bella sighed. "Right. Modesty is a human hang-up. They mentioned that a lot in the information sessions on the cruise. I forgot."

The steaks needed a few more minutes, so he busied himself filling two mugs with the liquor Bysshe brewed. He brought one over to Bella and offered it to her.

She sniffed at the liquor and then smiled. "Perfect. After the day I've had, I really need a drink. Wait a second... where did you get this from? You might have running water, but I'm certain you don't have a neighborhood bar."

"No bar, though we do meet up at the crash site at every month to drink and catch up. A friend of mine makes this stuff from fermented fruit. It's pretty good... for a plant."

Bella's gaze moved from the drink, to the steaks, and then to him. "Forgive me for asking, but does that mean dinner tonight is nothing but meat?"

The question confounded him. "What else would it be?"

"Um. Vegetables? Fruit?" She lifted the mug up. "Unfermented fruit, to be specific. I'm an omnivore. I eat both plants and animals."

"You eat *plants*?"

She mimicked his tone almost exactly and retorted, "You *don't* eat plants?"

"No. I eat what I hunt." He licked his lips, making sure

she noticed what he was doing. "But you already know that."

Color bloomed on her cheeks and she dropped her gaze. "Behave."

"Why would I do that? Teasing you is fun. I like watching your skin change colors." Despite his light words, he was concerned about what she'd told him. He didn't know much about the plant life, other than which ones to avoid and which ones Bysshe used to make his liquor. If Bella needed to eat the things, he was going to have to learn which ones were safe. Bysshe should be able to help. His creators were humans, so surely they'd programmed him with at least basic information about the species he was built to serve.

No one knew how Bysshe wound up under verexi ownership. He never talked about his former existence, and none of the fa'rel pushed him for details. His past didn't matter. His actions proved he was their stalwart ally and their friend.

"Tonight, meat. Tomorrow, I'll talk to Bysshe. He should know what plants you can eat. And I will bring fruit from his orchard for your next meal." He wrinkled his lip. "Just don't expect me to eat any of it."

"Bysshe? Who's that?"

"A friend. An android made by humans. He will want to meet you. So will the others once I tell them about you." He wasn't looking forward to that. He'd have to talk to Bysshe about finding some suitable clothes for Bella before he let the others near her. She was his. They could find their own females to admire.

That thought reminded him of something else. "You

mentioned other females. How many? Were they in the pods or with the main vessel?"

Bella's mouth turned down and her eyes were suddenly overflowing with water. "More of us, yes. I hope they made it. I don't know, though. Shit, I can't be the only one to make it. Some of the others had to make it to the pods."

She sucked in a quick breath and kept talking. "I think six of us were left onboard. We kept to ourselves most of the time. The few friends I made accepted offers from males along the way and left. I think it was the same for the others. It was hard to keep losing new friends, so I stopped trying."

She swiped at the water on her cheeks with the back of one hand. "I think we all felt a little foolish, being the last ones chosen. Seems petty now. I mean, I don't remember all their names and now they might be…"

He sat beside her on the bench and drew her gently into his lap. "Why are you leaking? Are you hurt?"

She tried to laugh but her voice cracked. "Sort of. My heart hurts because I'm sad. We shed tears when we feel like that." She pointed to her wet cheeks. "It helps flush out the stuff making us feel sad."

He kissed her face until the water was gone. He thought he understood at least a little of what she was feeling. She had survived when others hadn't. He knew that feeling. It kept him awake some nights, thinking of the ones who hadn't made it. Rage, Shatter, Ravage and all the others. Some had been gone for years, others only a few months. "We who remain will remember. Names are not important."

"How can you say that? Names matter."

"Some names do." He kissed the furrow between her

brows. "Others don't. The verexi only ever called me Subject Two. I chose my name for myself. Which one do you think matters to me?"

"You named yourself Mayhem? Why?"

"It was Rage's idea. He was our leader, even when we were young. He told us to pick a name for ourselves that would remind us what we'd do to the verexi if we had a chance to strike back."

"You wanted to rain mayhem and destruction down on them." Bella nodded. "I can understand that. You said Rage was your leader. He isn't anymore?"

"He died not long before we were sent here. Now, we don't have a leader. We make decisions together, as a clan."

She nodded and he sensed she was ready to talk about the others again.

"If the other females survived, my brothers will find them. Strife and Menace were here and saw the readouts. They set off on hunts of their own," he said.

She sniffed and turned her head so her cheek was pressed against his hand and then touched the marks on his chest. "Do you think this will happen to them, too?"

"I don't know. But I hope so. I'd like for them to find females of their own." Because if they did, they wouldn't look at Bella, and then he wouldn't have to kill them. Best they find their own females. Quickly.

He'd talk to Bysshe about that tomorrow, too.

"You said you saw readouts. Do you have tracking information? Trajectories? Why didn't you tell me that? We could be out looking right now!" She tried to stand, but he didn't let her.

"No. Nothing like that. It's more like an early warning

system, and even if we had that information, you are not going out there at night." He growled, needing her to hear him and understand. "Things out there are almost as dangerous as I am. You do not go out at night unless I'm with you."

She went still, and for a second he thought she was going to argue with him. Instead, she sighed, the sound heavy and tired. "Not without you," she repeated. "But the others. The ship. I need to know. Even if there's nothing to do but to bury their remains. I can do that much for them. Please?"

"I'll talk to Bysshe. He'll contact the others. The ship will be scavenged for parts and supplies, and the others will look for survivors."

"I want to be there," she said.

"Eventually. It's at least a day's run to reach the place I think it went down. My brothers will need to find it first. Once they do, I'll take you there."

"Thank you. I need to know what happened to them. We weren't close, but..." She shrugged.

He stayed with her a few minutes longer, letting her talk while he held her. Once she was calm again, he moved her back to the bench and went to serve their meal. She kept chatting, mostly about the females on her cruise. He knew what she was doing—gathering up recollections and small details so she could remember as much as she could. He and his brothers did the same thing.

She spoke of a younger female named Hope and one called Rissa. She mentioned other names, but Mayhem didn't try to remember them. If they were alive, he'd hear about them in the coming days.

Bella was more than half asleep by the time they finished eating. He tidied up quickly and then did something he'd only dreamed of.

He took his tired female to bed.

9

WAKING up to the sounds of nature was a new experience for Bella. She was a child of the city and rarely ventured past its walls in all the years she'd lived there.

Chitters, chirps, and trills filled the air, the volume increasing until she was dragged reluctantly to something resembling wakefulness. The only time she'd heard anything like this had been a recording that was supposed to improve her state of mind and make waking up easier. She'd deleted it after three days, so how was it playing again?

"Computer, turn off audio," she muttered once she was awake enough to form words. The noise didn't stop. "Dammit, audio off!"

She sat up, looked around, and remembered. It took a few seconds for everything to fall into place. Alarms, the crash, that disgusting slime, the strange orange and red forests of a new planet... and Mayhem. Holy hells. How had she forgotten about *him*?

Sunlight streamed through an open window and across the foot of the bed. She was nestled into one of the upper corners of the mattress with soft furs tucked in around her. One of the furs was folded into something like a pillow, and tucked in beside it was a small bouquet, the delicate blooms secured with a thong of leather.

He'd left her flowers. The air around her pillow was lightly perfumed with their scent, and she drew in a deep breath and smiled. Her demon had left her flowers.

She got up slowly, amused to note that even at her height, she had to hop down to the floor. It was built on a bigger scale than she was used to. The table had been higher, too, as were the stools. The furnishings made her feel almost petite in comparison.

She yawned and indulged herself in a thorough stretch, arms over her head, back arched. Her muscles protested at first. Between the crash landing and some of the most energetic sex she'd had in years, she felt a little battered and abused this morning.

Still, she'd slept well, and all in all, she felt pretty good. Maybe she wasn't too old for Mayhem and the way he lived after all. She rolled her shoulders and heard her neck crack in several places. Or maybe she was kidding herself. Still, it wasn't like she had many options.

She called for Mayhem but he didn't answer. Somewhere in the back of her mind she vaguely remembered him kissing her cheek and telling her that he was heading out to see his friend, Bysshe. "I'll be back as soon as I can, my falling star."

She was alone.

A sense of unease stuck to her as she freshened up in the bathroom. Being alone shouldn't have bothered her, but it did. She was used to being on her own, making decisions and doing what she thought was best with no one to second guess her... and no one else to help. How could she have become so reliant on one male in less than a day?

She answered her own question, speaking aloud to fill the quiet as she went through her ablutions, the cool water encouraging her to keep it quick. "Probably because I'm stuck on a prison planet, surrounded by a ridiculous number of trees that happen to be infested with all manner of things who want to get their first taste of human flesh."

Speaking of eating, she was hungry again. Ignoring how wildly inappropriate it was to make that leap in logic, she headed for the main room and what passed for a kitchen. She hadn't seen where Mayhem kept the meat he'd served last night. She'd expected to have to go looking, but he surprised her again. On the table was a plate with several slices of freshly cooked meat along with several dried sticks that turned out to be some kind of jerky. He'd left her another flower, too. And she added it to her bouquet before arranging them all in one of the mugs she found on a nearby shelf.

She poured herself some water from a wooden pitcher and then added some to the cup full of flowers and set it on the table. She didn't know when Mayhem had left, and she wasn't sure when he'd be back. The lack of information was strange. All her life she'd been in constant contact with the world around her. The datasphere kept her informed and entertained while vid calls and text messages let her stay connected to everyone in her network. The cruise had been quieter in some ways, but there'd still be information and updates coming in along with news from around the known galaxy.

Not anymore.

Now she was in a world without instant communication or rapid access to information. She looked around the table as she ate. Mayhem and his clan didn't even have paper, so he couldn't have left her a note.

Her whole life Bella had traded in information. It was the currency of her life, how she protected herself and provided for herself when no one else could be trusted to do it. She'd allied herself with other people in the same situation as she was. Companions and confidantes to the dangerous and powerful men who controlled their lives and most of the colony.

They'd built a network, trading information but never revealing too much or exposing their benefactors to too much scrutiny. No blackmail or gossip, just a careful exchange of tidbits and whispers that offered occasional financial opportunities. They had all gained from it. That's how she'd made enough to buy her way off Tova and onto that cruise ship.

And look where that had gotten her... stuck on a prison planet with no way off and no idea what to do now.

She puzzled over that problem while she ate. The jerky was so tough she gave up trying to cut it and settled for gnawing off a bit at a time and then washing it down with plenty of water. Even that tasted different here. It occurred to her it was the first time she'd ever had unfiltered water.

That's what this whole world was, unfiltered. Everything here was still raw, lacking the polish and pretense of polite civilization. Mayhem wanted her, so he'd taken her. He could have killed her instead, and nothing she could have done would have stopped him.

She rubbed at the marks on her wrists, watching to see if they faded. They didn't, but that didn't ease her worry much. She'd learned early on to lean into her strengths, and this place had stripped most of them away. She was too practical to pretend otherwise.

She knew her shortcomings and her strengths. What strengths she had didn't really matter here, not when her weaknesses were so problematic. Mayhem was her greatest hope for some kind of life, but what could she offer him in return. Sex? She knew that offer came with an expiry date. Men never stayed interested in that for long. At least, not from the same woman.

Mayhem seemed too good to be true. He was handsome, fit, brave, and determined to protect her. But for how long? The other women were still out there, most of them younger and more attractive than she had been, even in her heyday—a time so far in the past that the fashions of her youth had come back into style.

When he realized he had other choices, what reason would he have to stay with her?

She raised a hand in front of her, staring at the markings. Would they fade away? Why did she have them at all? It had to have something to do with Mayhem. The marks had appeared the same time as his. But like everything else, it seemed too good to be true. Bella had lived too long to take anything at face value... even if she wanted him to be right.

But nothing was ever that simple.

With breakfast eaten and her single plate cleaned and put with the others, Bella ran out of things to do besides worry about something she couldn't do a damned thing about. She opted to explore what was, at least for now, her new home.

Wandering around someone else's house felt odd. Doing it naked felt wrong on levels she couldn't explain, even to herself. She felt better after tracking down the same leather kilt Mayhem had let her borrow last night. The straps didn't hide everything, but it was better than nothing. "If you're going to live here, you're going to need to let go of a few things, like clothes." She thought about Mayhem's reactions to her request for vegetables and sighed. "And carbs. If they don't eat plants, there's no chance of fresh bread in my future."

She wandered out onto the deck, exploring each of the smaller buildings in turn. One was for storage and held a bewildering collection of items. Tools, some handmade, some clearly manufactured. Piles of screws, nails, and other building supplies filled the shelves. The rest was a jumble of items she didn't recognize, though clearly they mattered to Mayhem.

The next room made her stop and stare. It was full of tech, and if the flashing lights she saw weren't figments of her imagination, it all worked. Not that she had any idea what it did. Two monitors sat on a simple table. One showed nothing but readouts. The other had to be how he'd known about the pods and the crashing ship. It was a sensor array. She'd seen a few of them on vids and once when they'd taken a tour of the cruise ship's command deck. Mayhem hadn't been lying to her, though. She could see it was cobbled together from different systems. It wasn't going to show her where the others were. It wasn't even strong enough to indicate where her pod had landed.

Her pod wasn't going to be much use to anyone, but the emergency supplies might give her something to barter with. Even though Mayhem had already laid claim to everything, it had been hers first. Sort of. And she'd like to go back to retrieve the rations. They'd probably taste horrible, but they'd have vitamins and minerals she needed until they could work out what plants were safe for her to eat.

She'd need Mayhem's help to find the pod again. Hells, she needed his help with everything.

Frustrated and on edge, she moved further into the shed. Fans blew a steady stream of air over the various machines to stop them overheating. Fans, the early warning systems, the glow-pods, and who knew what other gadgets all needed power. So, where the hells was it coming from?

It didn't take long to find the power cords. They were gathered in a neat bundle, all of them leading down to a hole in the floor. She couldn't see where they went after that, which meant she needed a new perspective. If looking down didn't work, she'd try looking up.

The stairs seemed steeper without Mayhem there to steady her. It didn't help that watching where she put her feet meant looking down. If this was really going to be her new home, they'd need to put up a guide rail or maybe an elevator.

She hadn't noticed the small landing yesterday. It wasn't large, but it was large enough to let her walk under the deck. That's where she saw the batteries. They were secured beneath the floor by two rows of brackets, one on either side of the small landing. Several bundles of smaller wires fed into them from above, but only one main power line led down. She followed it.

The line was strung from tree to tree, high enough to be out of the way but still accessible. She walked beneath it, grateful that Mayhem had remembered to retrieve her shoes yesterday.

Had it really only been a day ago? Or had it been less than that? She'd lost track of time already, another problem she'd never experienced before. She had no way to tell time on this world, at least, none she could use. Mayhem could probably tell by sniffing the wind or seeing where the sun was in the sky. Without access to the datasphere, she had no idea.

The power line led down to the river, though not to the pool they'd swum in yesterday. It went further upriver. Even before she reached the end, she knew what she'd find. The river narrowed, forcing the water to move faster as it churned between the rocks with enough force to make the whole area into a single, fast-moving set of rapids.

Several micro hydro-generators were visible below the frothing surface. Hydroelectricity. That's where their power came from. Gathered here and stored in the batteries they'd liberated from the wreckage and whatever supplies the verexi had dumped here. That part niggled at her. If they planned on killing Mayhem and the others, why send supplies at all? For that matter, why take them anywhere? They were already prisoners. They didn't need to do any of this... unless they were trying to convince someone they really intended to free the fa'rel. But who would that be and why?

She didn't have enough information to make even a

wild guess, but she kept turning it over in her head anyway. She took a seat near the river, careful not to get too close to the edge. She was close enough to the clearing to hear if Mayhem came back and called for her, and the river threw up a light mist that kept the air a little cooler than it had been at the house. The sounds of the river blended with the hum and chatter of the local wildlife to create a comfortable sort of white noise. It was a good place to sit and think.

The setting was pretty, but after twenty minutes or so Bella decided to head back. Cooler air and a nice view didn't make up for the fact her ass was going numb from sitting on a cold, lumpy boulder.

She was on her feet, waiting for the pins and needles to subside when it dawned on her that something was different. Her instincts screamed, and she turned in place, trying to see what had changed. Everything looked the same, but the feeling that something was wrong intensified.

The woods were quiet. No, not quiet. *Silent.* The river was the only thing making any noise.

Bella balled her hands into fists, squared her shoulders, and set off for the treehouse at a steady pace. She didn't know much about nature, but she knew all about predators. If she ran, whatever was out there would chase her.

"Fuck," she muttered to herself as she fought her rising fear. "Fuck, fuck, fuck. Whatever you are, go find something else to eat for lunch. I'm old and tough and full of gristle. You can do better. Trust me."

Something hissed from up ahead of her. She froze, but then something else moved from her left. *Shit.* She had at least two of whatever the fuck was out there to deal with. She had no idea what to do, so she followed her instincts.

Not the one to run, but the other one. The one that screamed at her to get *away*.

"Most predators big enough to bother us can't climb that high." That's what Mayhem had said.

She bolted for the nearest tree and clambered up its twisted and gnarled trunk as fast as she could. She lost a shoe but kept going, trying not to think about what was making all the ruckus at the foot of the tree—angry hissing noises and the scrabble of claws on wood. She kept climbing until she ran out room and then wedged herself into a crook between two massive branches.

Only then did she allow herself to look down. Two massive creatures circled the base of the tree. They were as long as Mayhem was tall with thick, heavy bodies, stocky legs, and massive claws. Their hides were scaly, mostly black but with orange and red patches that must work as camouflage. One of them looked up at her and hissed, jaws opening to reveal a massive maw as black as night but no teeth. For a brief second she felt relief. No teeth had to be a good sign. Right?

That little bubble of hope burst like a soap bubble hitting a fan when the lizard-thing moved again. *Shit*. It did have teeth. A lot of them. Big, sharp, and as jet-black as its mouth.

Strips torn out of the bark showed her how far they'd managed to get before their weight had made it impossible for them to climb any higher. Her perch was less than a meter higher up, but she was safe for the moment.

That's when the other creatures came into view. They were smaller, faster, and their coloring was lighter. Fucking hells, it was a family... and those smaller ones looked like they could climb better than their full-grown parents.

She filled her lungs and started yelling. If Mayhem didn't get back soon, she wouldn't have to worry about him losing interest. She'd be too dead to care.

10

Despite their need for space, none of them lived too far from the others in case of trouble. Mayhem's territory along with all the others were laid out in a pattern based around a central point—the crash site. Every clan needed a meeting place, and that was theirs. It was also Bysshe's home.

The sky was clear, the air still carrying a hint of freshness after last night's storm, and the surrounding woods were alive with the twitter of green-backed lizards and several avian-type animals no one had bothered to name yet. The next time he made this walk he should bring Bella. This area was too well-traveled to provide good hunting for him or any of this planet's predators.

He liked the idea of walking with Bella, showing her his world and teaching her about its beauties and its dangers. He wanted to share his life with her and have someone to talk to about the little things that filled his days. That wasn't something he'd ever expected to have. He loved his clan brothers, but they couldn't stay too long in each other's company or tempers would fray. It was part of their nature. Bysshe had explained that they were all dominant personalities. When no one was willing to back down, fights were inevitable.

That's one of the reasons the scrawnies had separated them once they reached puberty. It also prevented them from making cohesive plans. How could they work together when they were never allowed to see each other?

It had been years since he'd seen more than one or two of his clan mates at a time. When they'd all been crowded into the hold of the ship that brought them here, the atmosphere had quickly become one of celebration and joyful reunion. It hadn't lasted, though. Within days they were all on edge and snarling at each other. Part of it was knowing they'd be fighting for their lives soon, but that wasn't the only reason. The verexi had crammed them all into the hold and locked them in there with no access to the rest of the ship. They had minimal comforts and sufficient food but no privacy. Most likely their captors had hoped there'd be enough chaos and infighting on the journey to keep everyone distracted.

It hadn't worked. They hadn't been together for years, but they were still a clan, and their survival was at stake.

Being with Bella was different. She didn't rile him up. In fact, she was like a cool swim on a hot day, blissful and soothing. He grinned, recalling yesterday's encounter in the river. Soothing wasn't the right word for what she'd done to him... or what he'd done to her. Satisfying was closer, but it wasn't strong enough. He'd have to take her swimming again this afternoon and see if he could find the right words after they'd done it again.

Finding her had changed everything. She'd slept beside him, falling asleep without doubt or hesitation. She didn't fear him. In fact, she trusted him to protect her while she was at her most vulnerable. He didn't want to go back to a life without her, and he'd kill anyone or anything that threatened to take her from him.

Thoughts of Bella spurred him to move faster. He was already jogging, but he broke into a ground-covering lope that would get him there faster. He'd had enough of being on his own. He wanted to be with Bella. The sooner he talked to Bysshe, the sooner he'd be home.

The trees thinned out as he reached the edge of the crash site. Nature had been busy replacing and repairing what the ship had damaged, but the destruction had been extensive. The ship had carved a swath through the forest before it finally slammed into the base of a hill, partially burying itself in the process.

New growth had sprouted and was slowly re-covering the forest floor, but it would be a few more years before most of the damage was erased. They'd transplanted some saplings around the ship to shield it from view, but they couldn't hide it completely. It might be partially buried, but it would still show up on most orbital scans. The wind turbines were hard to miss, too.

All three of them were visible from where he stood, the blades hand forged and the towers little more than scrap metal held together by welds, rivets, and hope. They weren't pretty, but they worked well enough. Together they produced a good portion of the power needed to run what was left of the crashed ship's systems. The rest came from micro hydro-generators that did most of the work during the rainy season.

This close, he could hear the creak and thrum of the turbines along with one that had developed a squeak. Yesterday's storm had probably done some minor damage. It would need to be repaired and rebalanced before long. Bysshe maintained most of the site himself, but he usually left the turbine repairs to one of the fa'rel. The android was more than capable, but Mayhem and his clansmen were better climbers and had the greater reach.

Finding Bysshe wasn't difficult. He might move quietly and produce very little scent, but his coloring made him stand out. He was the only bald, blue humanoid on the planet, after all, and he was in his favorite spot—his orchard. At least, that's what they all called it. In reality it was only a small grove of fruit-bearing trees Bysshe had located, tagged, and then asked the others to help him dig them up and carry back to the clearing. None of the fa'rel ate the fruit, though they all appreciated the liquor Bysshe brewed from it.

Rows of planters acted as a sort of fence to the grove, all of them full of plants Bysshe believed were medicinal. They'd be important in the long term because their stash of medical supplies was limited. There'd been a few med-kits on the ship and a handful of first-aid packs had been tossed in with the supplies left for them, but it wasn't going to be enough. Some of it was verexi specific, some medicines were expired, and every kit was incomplete.

Mayhem and the others all healed quickly and had been inoculated against a wide variety of pathogens to keep them healthy. That had made the issue less concerning, but that had all changed. Now they had the females to consider.

Judging by the scrapes Bella had still shown this morning, it was obvious they didn't heal quickly. His female and the others were vulnerable... and that was unacceptable.

The thought of Bella in pain or hurt made him want to snarl in frustration. Bysshe would know what to do. He always did, or if he wasn't sure, he'd admit it and they'd find a way forward together. The android had been with them since they were young. He was their mentor, a secret ally, and the one the verexi used to communicate with their creations most of the time. The scrawnies never interacted with them unless the fa'rel were safely confined or restrained... with good reason.

"Bysshe!" Mayhem called out.

Bysshe was gathering fruit and turned toward Mayhem, a basket in one arm half full of the day's offerings. "Mayhem! What brings you here? I saw the flare. Are you bringing news, or were you hurt during yesterday's hunt?"

"The hunt?" It took Mayhem a second to remember. Right, he thought the incoming ships were part of another attack. He'd sent up the flare... and sent his brothers running to meet something none of them had expected.

He grinned to himself. He hoped their *hunts* had gone as well has his.

"The ships weren't attackers. They were escape pods."

He told Bysshe about Bella, the other pods, and the crashed ship.

His first question wasn't the one Mayhem expected. "Humans are here. On this planet?" Bysshe's normally placid expression had shifted into something else, though it was still unreadable to Mayhem.

"There are. *Female* humans."

"Indeed. And you said the one you found gave you those marks? How?" He pointed to the strange marks that crisscrossed Mayhem's chest.

"I don't know how. They appeared after I mated with her." Fuck, in his hurry to share everything he'd forgotten to tell Bysshe everything. "She has these marks too, but on her wrists. They weren't there before, but afterward…"

For the first time Mayhem could recall, the android was speechless. His mouth fell open, but no words came out, and then he closed it again with a click. His eyes got a distant look that usually meant he was accessing his internal database.

Mayhem waited in silence.

It wasn't more than a minute before Bysshe was back and aware again. "Humans are a most surprising species."

"Why?" Mayhem didn't like it when Bysshe was cryptic. He preferred straightforward facts.

The android set down the basket he carried and then moved into a stance they were all familiar with. Feet apart, shoulders back, hands crossed at the wrists behind his back. He and the others called it "teacher mode." Mayhem sighed inwardly and slouched against the nearest tree. So much for straightforward.

"How much do you know about humans?"

Mayhem cocked his head to one side and offered his mentor a lopsided grin. "Whatever you told us, plus a few images from vids."

"Ah. Well, they weren't a species you were expected to encounter. There aren't that many of them, and they're scattered across the galaxy. The one thing you should know is that they are one of the few species that can interbreed.

Not with every other species, of course, but several of them. A quirk of genetics perhaps, or proof that humans are the end result of an ancient attempt at planetary seeding."

"So the reason all the females on this mating cruise were human is because they're compatible breeding partners for other species?

"Quite likely. It's one of the reasons the Galactic Legion tolerates them. It's also why

they haven't died out, despite the fact they were—I believe the term is *late to the party*. They had enough knowledge and tech to fly out to the stars, but they weren't prepared for what they found once they got there. Their first encounters with the legion were not pleasant ones."

This was all new to Mayhem. "How do you know that?"

Bysshe raised one shoulder in a slight shrug. "I am older than I look."

That was enough information for now. "Do you know what they eat? Bella says she needs more than just meat."

"She's correct." He pointed to the basket he'd been filling. "She can eat anything in there. Take some and I'll leave the rest for the other females. You're the first to find one, but from what you've told me, you won't be the last."

"She asked me about clothes. Her skin is so soft she's going to need some way to protect it."

"Indeed. I use a small fabricator to create my garments. It has a significant power requirement and there's a limited amount of raw material, but I've been working on possible alternatives. I'll begin making what the humans will need."

Mayhem nodded. "Thank you. I want her to be protected." He also wanted her well-covered when she was near any of his brothers.

"Once you're gone, I'll visit some of the others. Those who found no one in their territory will want to go for the main ship."

"No doubt. None of them will miss out on a chance to find a female of their own." Mayhem grabbed an assortment of fruit from the basket Bysshe had indicated and stashed them in a bag he had slung over one shoulder.

"You want to get back to her." It wasn't a question, but Mayhem answered anyway.

"I do. I can't explain it, but it doesn't feel right when I am away from her."

"Interesting." Bysshe's gaze dropped to the marks on Mayhem's chest. "Next time you come, bring your female. I'd like to meet her and hear more about the bond developing between you."

"I'll bring her soon."

"I look forward to meeting her."

Mayhem walked out of sight of the clearing before he broke into a run. No need to let Bysshe know how eager he was to get back to Bella. He couldn't wait to give her the fruit and reassure her that the others would soon be going to look for more survivors.

The distance flew by, and it felt like no time at all before he was almost home. That's when he heard Bella screaming for him.

He followed the sound at a dead sprint, claws out, fangs bared, and fury coursing through his veins. Something was threatening his female. That something was about to die.

11

"Fuck off and find something else for lunch!" Bella had a broken off branch in one hand, her remaining shoe in the other, and was using them both to fend off the smaller lizards as they tried to reach her.

They were tenacious little beasts. No matter how many times she knocked them off the tree, they came back to try again. Worse, she was tiring, and the lizards clung to the bark like they had superglue on their claws.

Eventually, one of them was going to reach her. Four of them were working in concert, and she only had two hands.

She yelled for Mayhem every chance she got, but her voice was getting hoarse, and she didn't know how far the noise would carry. She didn't know how long she'd been up this damned tree, either. It might have only been a few minutes, though it felt like hours.

"Mayhem!" she screamed again as one of the lizard things charged her. She swatted it with her shoe, hoping to dislodge it. Instead, the cursed creature attacked, sinking claws and fangs into her footwear.

"Shit! Let go!" Her voice rose an octave as her fear escalated into something closer to terror. She flailed, desperately trying to shake the lizard loose. She even tried slamming it against the branches, but it glared at her and held on.

The others moved in, sensing her distraction. If she stayed focused on one of them, the rest would reach her.

"Fuck off already!" She whipped her hand back, still holding on to her shoe, and then hurled overhand with all her strength. Footwear and lizard both went flying. She didn't bother to watch where they landed. She had more immediate concerns. She grabbed the branch held with both hands and shook it at the remaining creatures. "You come any closer and you'll be airborne, too."

"Mayhem! Help!" she called out again, desperately hoping he'd be back soon. She was running out of time.

A roar tore through the forest, followed by the sound of something charging through the woods. Something much scarier than the lizards was coming. She really hoped it was Mayhem out there. If it wasn't...

The adult lizards froze for a second. They started frantically chittering at their offspring. Two of them abandoned the hunt and scrambled down the tree to rejoin their parents. One didn't. Bella tightened her grip on the branch and waited for it to make the first move.

Mayhem's arrival was something to behold. From her vantage point, she spotted him a second or two before the lizards on the ground did. He ran faster than she would have thought possible, and before she could blink, he was at the foot of the tree.

The two adults attacked while the smaller ones bolted

for safety. The air filled with the sounds of furious fighting —snarls and hisses and the sound of tearing flesh. Some of the sounds changed from fury to pain. She hoped Mayhem was the one dealing out the damage, not taking it himself.

Distracted by the fight below, she forgot about the last juvenile. The little bastard hadn't forgotten about her, though. It came at her again, and this time she was too slow.

It was on her before she could swat it with the branch, and she dropped the makeshift weapon to beat at the creature with her bare hands. Claws raked, fangs slashed, but the leather kilt she'd donned that morning protected her from the worst of the damage. The lizard didn't understand what armor was and attacked it as if it were part of her.

She managed to knock it off at one point. It fell to a lower branch, gathered itself and was about to come at her again when a knife suddenly appeared in its back, pinning it to the tree.

It thrashed and squealed, and then Mayhem was there. He stabbed it with a second blade and it went still. Then he looked up at her.

She'd never been so happy to see anyone in her life. "You came," she said, her voice raw and shakier than she would have liked. Showing weakness was something she'd learned never to do, but right now she couldn't help it.

"Always, my Bella. Are you hurt?"

"Just scratches I think. Maybe a few splinters. You?"

"They never touched me." He held out a hand to her. "Come here."

She leaned down far enough to take his offered hand. It was stained and wet with what had to be blood, but right now she didn't care.

He helped her down part of the way and then wrapped her in his arms to make the leap to the ground. He didn't set her down right away. Instead, he carried her far enough she couldn't see or smell the bodies of the creatures he'd killed. Then he set her down gently, though she could feel the tension in his muscles. He was still keyed up from the fight. So was she, for the moment, but she knew the adrenaline crash would come soon. Her hands were shaking and she felt jittery and off balance already.

He kissed her softly, holding her close, his arms wrapped around her as if he'd never let her go. She let herself lean into him, borrowing his strength. "I've got you, Bella. You're safe."

Once her breathing slowed and her hands steadied, he loosened his hold on her without letting her go completely. He moved his hands over her body, checking every inch of her and making note of every injury, no matter how minor. He touched the leather straps of his kilt that fell over her body and smiled. "I will need that back eventually. I'll have to make you one of your own."

"Yes, please. I'd like to learn how to make them, too. I want to be useful. I just..." She gestured to herself and then at him. "I've got nothing to offer you right now. I'd like to change that."

"Nothing to offer?" Mayhem cocked his head, the dark lines above his eyes creasing in thought. "You think your only value to me is in what you can do?"

"Well, yeah. That's how the world works."

He growled softly. "That was how your world worked. You're in mine now."

Something in his tone made her heart fill with the most

dangerous emotion of all... hope. "And how do things work here?"

"I don't care who you were before or what skills you have. I'll teach you what I know, and we'll learn more together." He kissed her brow. "We've only been here a year. There's still much my clan has to learn about this place. You'll learn, too."

He pointed down to her bare feet. "We'll start by teaching you not to throw your shoes at anything that attacks you."

She kept her head bowed as she argued. "Technically I didn't throw it *at* anything. I threw it away because a lizard was chewing on the toe."

"No more throwing your shoes. I'll show you how to throw knives instead."

"And if I suck at it? What if I'm no good at any of this?" The moment the words were out of her mouth she recognized that was what she was truly afraid of. If she couldn't adapt to life here, would he still want her? Or would she become a burden he came to resent?

All humor left his voice and he caught her chin in one hand, forcing her to look up at him. "You will learn. But if you can't master some skills, someone else in the clan will help. Do you think I know how to do everything? I don't. The verexi only taught us how to be soldiers. To hunt, hurt, and kill. Do you think that makes me less valuable?"

"Of course not!"

"Then why don't you see yourself that way?" he demanded.

She tried to look away, but he didn't let her. To her horror, her eyes welled up with tears and she felt a jagged flash of pain deep in her soul. A dark, ugly truth flowed out of that wound, and for the first time in her life she let herself acknowledge it and give it a name. "Because that's all I've been to anyone until now. No value except for what I could give them. Information. Connections. Status." She swallowed hard and then added the last word. "Sex."

There. She'd said it. Now he knew it all.

He pulled her in tightly against him, tucking her head down so it fit beneath his chin.

She pressed her face against the soft fur of his chest and waited for his next words.

"I don't care, Bella. That was your world. I want you to live in mine."

She blew out a long breath and closed her eyes. "I want that, too."

"Good. Now we have that settled, I'm taking you home." She laughed softly and nodded. "Home sounds good. Please tell me those lizard things can't climb that high."

He swung her into his arms and set off for the treehouse, cradling her against his chest like she was the most precious thing in all the worlds. It was a feeling she was learning to love.

"We call them Black Fangs, and the adults cannot climb much at all. The juveniles can, but they don't go very high unless they see obvious prey. We build our homes too far off the ground for them to reach."

"Thank the stars for that. I think I'm going to stay up in our tree until I learn how to kill those things... and get better footwear."

"Bysshe is already working on that. And I will talk to

one of my brothers who is good with leather. You will be well protected."

"I already am." She patted his shoulder. "I have you. Oh, I didn't even say thank you yet. If you hadn't come back when you did, we wouldn't be having this conversation."

He snarled. "I know. It was a near thing. I didn't know that pack had moved into my territory or I would not have left you alone. I'll go back later today, retrieve your shoes and deal with the bodies."

"We're not eating them. Are we?" She wasn't sure how she felt about that. As revenge went, it seemed fitting, but they hadn't looked all that appetizing either.

"No. They're too tough and taste terrible. Their skins are useful though." He glanced down at her bare feet. "In fact, I think I know what your first pair of shoes will be made of."

She kissed his cheek, feeling happier and more hopeful than she'd ever been before. With those feelings came other ones... carnal and heated. "That is an excellent idea, but it will have to wait until much later. After we're cleaned up, I have other plans for you."

He growled and the sound rolled into that low, repetitive rumble that was almost like a purr. "Who said anything about waiting until *after*?"

12

———

THIS TIME she didn't have to navigate the stairs herself. Mayhem carried her all the way to the bathroom, barely slowing down as he raced up the stairs. She closed her eyes and held on.

She didn't open them again until they were inside. She found herself back on her feet as her lover moved around the room, turning on the glow-pods with one hand while he pulled off what little he'd been wearing. Weapons and leather straps fell to the floor, along with a bag he set down carefully in one corner. She didn't know what was in it, and before she could ask about it, he turned to her and whisked the leather kilt over her head.

His lips crashed down on hers, hungry and demanding. She surrendered to him instinctively, letting him take control. After the day she'd had, she was happy to let someone else be in charge.

She needed this. Needed him. The touch of his hands, the taste of his mouth, and the warm bulk of his body eclipsed everything else. He guided her to the shower, reaching out blindly to slap at the lever. It took him a few seconds to turn on the shower, and then they were standing under a downpour of cool water.

His cock was already hard and ready, a thick bar pressed against her stomach. She tried to ignore her needs to see to his. She scooped out a bit of the soft goo they used as cleanser and worked it into a lather between her hands the way Mayhem had showed her last night. He did the same for her, mirroring her actions, both of them teasing the other and getting teased in return.

She saved the best for last, working her way down to his feet before coming up to cup his balls in one hand.

"Yes," he hissed between clenched teeth as she wrapped her other hand around the thick length of his cock.

She eased herself onto her knees without letting go of him. He tensed, his eyes widening as he realized what she intended to do.

"Bet your pleasure bots couldn't do this," she said and leaned forward to take the tip of his cock into her mouth. He groaned and shuddered. "More of that."

She pulled away and lifted her head to look at him. He'd reached up to turn off the water and then braced one hand against the wall. His claws were out, the tips digging into the wood.

He looked incredible. "More of this?" she asked and then opened her mouth and took in as much of him as she could.

He groaned again, the ridges on his cock pulsing along her tongue. She caressed his balls and hummed, keeping him deep in the heat of her mouth.

His thighs tensed until she could see the lines of muscle

clearly. His hand dropped to the top of her head, stroking her hair. She experimented, swiping her tongue over the tip of his cock and then taking him deep and stroking the rest of him with her fingers as she learned what he liked best.

She didn't stop until he was gasping, that sexy-as-fuck purring sound rising from his chest. "Stop. I need... I need to be inside you when I come."

She didn't stop right away. It was intoxicating to have him at her mercy like this, and she kept it up for another minute before finally letting go.

The moment he was out of her mouth he had her by one wrist, helping her to her feet and then hauling her out of the bathing room and back to their bedroom.

"On the bed. Hands and knees. Now."

She obeyed him, wondering if he knew that his tone of voice had made her shiver as a dark thrill chased down her spine. She'd played the part of the meek and attentive companion when necessary, but she'd never truly submitted to anyone before. She'd always retreated into the small part of herself she kept hidden, but with Mayhem, she didn't have to hide. She knew that now. He wanted her for who she was, not what she could do for him. He didn't care about her age, her abilities, or her past. He wanted *her*.

He stood behind her, one hand splayed across her back as he reached between her legs with the other. His fingers caressed the seam of her pussy before pushing inside. She arched her back and moaned, rocking against his questing fingers until he found what she needed most. Her clit throbbed as he drew a circle around it with one fingertip, and she managed a decent imitation of his growl as she threw him a warning look over her shoulder. "Flirt later. Fuck now."

His eyes burned like twin suns as he flicked his finger over the swollen knot of flesh buried in her folds. "If you want something, female, ask me for it."

She held his gaze and managed to keep her voice steady and moan-free. "I need you, Mayhem. Please. Make me come."

"Whatever my Bella needs, she can have." He worked her clit with the roughened pads of his fingers, stroking it faster and faster. She dropped her head and moaned, every touch making her shiver as he pushed her to the brink of release. Just as she was about to break, he withdrew his hand, leaving her frustrated and panting with need.

He didn't make her wait long.

He gripped her hip in one hand and positioned his cock with the other, lining up and then sliding into her in one fluid thrust. Her body gave way to his, her inner walls flexing around him and drawing him deeper inside.

He didn't stop until he was fully sheathed with no room between them. She expected him to take her hard, but he didn't move. Instead, he asked her a question. "Who am I?"

"Mayhem," she replied, not sure where this was leading.

"What am I?" Ah. Now she understood. The answer fell from her lips as easily as breathing. "My male." She glanced back at him. "My protector. My everything."

"Yes." He lowered himself until her his chest brushed her back and he had to steady himself with one hand planted on the mattress beside hers.

"Your everything, always. And you..." He finally

withdrew, only to drive himself in even deeper with his next thrust. "Are mine."

"Yes," she whispered, the word fading into a moan. "I am."

Bella abandoned herself to the storm swirling inside her. She crested each wave of pleasure only to find herself rising on a new one that took her even higher. Mayhem's warm breath fanned over the skin of her back. The ridges on his cock began to flare, intensifying her pleasure.

He nipped the top of her shoulder and she shivered as that small moment of pain blended with the ecstasy of the moment.

Then, his teeth closed on her shoulder again. He didn't break the skin, using only enough strength to hold her in place as he chased his own release, taking her with him.

He sped up again, every stroke bringing her closer to orgasm. It was wild, and wanton, and so perfect she never wanted it to end. But then her orgasm hit and nothing else mattered but the pleasure coursing through her... and the male who had given it to her.

She came hard, calling out his name as her world exploded into shards of crystalline bliss. Her body tightened around him, and he released her shoulder to throw back his head and roar as he came. He thrust once more, burying himself to the hilt inside her as jet after jet of cum filled her. She sucked in a quick breath, knowing what would happen next. The ridges on his cock flared fully, locking him inside her and pushing her into another orgasm.

It was perfect.

Afterward they spooned on the bed, his bigger frame wrapped around hers. The events of the day had caught up to her, leaving her tired and too weary to move. Mayhem had taken care of her, even bringing in a plate of fresh fruit and cool water before curling up beside her and telling her about his visit with Bysshe.

She felt sated, safe, and happy. *Truly* happy. It was the best feeling in the galaxy. And all she had to do to find it was crash on a prison planet and fall in love with a demon who threatened to kill her the first time they met.

She snorted softly to herself, making Mayhem stir.

"What is it?" he asked.

"I was just reminded that the universe is run by assholes and nothing is ever easy."

He grunted and nuzzled her hair. "I could have told you that. Sleep, my falling star. You need to recover your strength."

She closed her eyes and snuggled closer to him. If this was what the rest of her life would be like, she couldn't wait to get started.

EPILOGUE

So much had changed since the first time she'd seen this place, but the pool of water where she and Mayhem had first made love still looked the same... mostly.

"Aunty Bella. Watch this!" the piping voice of one of Hope's twins, she had no idea which one, drew Bella's attention.

One of the boys played in the shallows, which were now separated from the deeper areas by a ring of stones. The one who had called to her to watch was on the shore, almost aglow with potential mischief. He had the same markings as his father, though his fur was a deeper shade of gold, and he had his mother's blue eyes.

The moment he had her attention, he charged into the water as fast as he could and threw himself forward in an impressive belly flop, arms and legs splayed out to make the biggest splash he could manage.

"No running!" Hope yelled at her son and then sighed as she realized he couldn't hear her. He was still thrashing around in the water.

The three women were all seated near the shallows, basking in the afternoon sun, feet dangling in the water as they watched the children play. They'd been mere acquaintances once, but they were her best friends now. Rissa and Hope were the sisters she'd never had growing up. Their lives had changed so much since the crash, but Bella had embraced the changes, and so had her friends.

None of them would go back to the lives they'd had before.

Rissa drained her glass of juice and then nodded in the direction of the treehouse. "How long do you think we have?"

Bella laughed and then glanced up at the sun, estimating how long the males had been working. "Until they finish repairing that fence? Probably another hour. But they'll be driving each other crazy by now. Any minute they're going to descend on us and havoc will ensue."

Rissa snickered. "Don't you mean Mayhem? If your mate hears you speak another male's name, he's going to get all snarly."

"It's not my fault he and Havoc have names that mean the same thing," Bella shrugged. "Besides, he'll be all snarly anyway. You know what they're like when they spend too long in each other's company." She flexed her hands into claws and curled her upper lip back to flash her teeth at the other women. "Grr, grr, rawr. I'm a fa'rel male and I'm in charge."

All three of them laughed, and Hope raised her mug of juice in mock salute. "Or at least that's what we let them think."

That had them all chortling again, their merriment

drifting on the afternoon breeze. Bella knew it was loud enough their males would hear them and come to investigate, but that was fine. The repairs to the garden fence could wait. She'd been away from Mayhem long enough. They'd been together for several years now, but she still felt her heart race every time he walked into view. The bond between them had only deepened over time, and now they couldn't bear to be parted for more than a few hours.

Hope looked at her twins with love and a hint of worry. "I hope the next generation doesn't share that part of their fathers' nature. Puberty is going to be hard enough as it is without them at each other's throats because they all want to be charge. There's only so much growling I can take. And if they try to boss their dad around..." Hope shook her head. "He'll lose his mind, and I'll be right there with him."

"It won't happen for years, if it happens at all." Bella smiled at the younger woman. "Mayhem and I talked about it already, though. If you need to split the boys up eventually, we'll be happy to take one of them. That way they'll be close to home but with enough space to keep everyone mostly sane."

"I hope that isn't necessary, but thank you. It's nice to know we'd have that option. Do you think Mayhem would really be okay with having a hormonal teen boy around?"

"Oh, we talked about that, too." Bella grinned. "His plan is to toss the lad into this pool every time he gets too pushy."

"That... might work."

Further conversation was interrupted by the appearance of three naked figures racing across the clearing to the water's edge. Mayhem, Strife, and Menace were clearly racing because all three of them were throwing elbows and doing their best to trip up the other two as they ran.

"They never change," Rissa murmured and rolled her eyes, but she had a smile in her voice as she said it.

"I hope mine never does," Bella said.

"Me too," Hope said.

"Me three," Rissa added.

The twins noticed the new arrivals, splashing the water and calling out encouragement to their dad.

Bella didn't care who made it to the water first. In her eyes, Mayhem was always the winner. He'd been the one to win her heart, and now he was her male, her protector, her everything.

***

Thank You for Reading Marked For Mayhem

Want to read Rissa and Mayhem's special bonus epilogue? Sign up for my newsletter

www.subscribepage.com/crashedandclaimed

And if you want to know how Mayhem's friends are doing, you're welcome to explore the rest of the series... starting with Marked For Strife.

BONUS CONTENT - MARKED FOR RAGE

The print copy of Marked For Mayhem also includes the prequel story for this series - Marked for Rage.

I hope you enjoy it!
Susan

ABOUT THE BOOK

It was supposed to be a delivery run... How did it turn into a prison break?

All Mercy had to do was deliver her cargo and go. Now she's got a bunch of irate aliens on her tail and a hot-as-Helios escaped prisoner in her cargo bay who insists she is *his*. She's too old for this crap, and she keeps telling herself she's too old for him, too. But his arguments and his... assets are very convincing.

If they're going to survive this intergalactic crisis, she's going to need a plan... and her hot, horned, and handsome alien passenger is going to need some clothes.

**Buckle up. This sci-fi romance contains an alien with fur, fangs, horns, and a very possessive attitude when it comes to the woman he's claimed for his own.

1

RAGE

THE GUARDS TOSSED Rage through the door with no care for how he landed, which meant his head slammed into the floor so hard he saw stars. By the time his vision cleared, the door to his cell had slammed shut, leaving him in total darkness. Not that he needed to see to know his surroundings intimately. He'd been here many times.

The isolation wing. *Again.*

He didn't try to get up. The effect of the stun weapons they'd hit him with hadn't worn off yet. If he attempted to move before they were gone, he'd only make the recovery time longer, and it was painful enough as it was.

The cell was barely long enough for him to lie flat on the floor and high enough that he could reach the ceiling by stretching out his hands while standing. One long wall had a narrow platform built into it that could be used as either a bench or a bed. He only fit on it if he slept on his side and didn't move much, so he normally slept on the floor. He'd been here often enough to know the routine, and so did the vermin that lived in this part of the complex. They'd learned long since that if they didn't disturb him, he'd refrain from tearing their heads off and leaving their corpses as a warning to the others.

A small sink and sanitation area sat on the back wall but nothing else of note. Certainly nothing that could be used as a weapon. The verexi had learned that lesson years ago. Rage and the rest of his clan were dangerous all on their own. If given access to anything that could be used as a weapon, the results were... messy.

He grinned a little, knowing that no one could see him right now. His captors would turn on the light once he was on his feet. Until then, he enjoyed the respite from constant surveillance. He'd only allow himself this short time to acknowledge pain while he was hidden, shielded by darkness with no chance they could see his expression. He would never give the scrawnies that satisfaction. Never. It was the only win he could claim in a lifetime of losses.

As he basked in the anonymous darkness, he reflected on his current situation. The escape attempt had failed, but he'd managed to spend some time exploring and adding to his knowledge of the area beyond their cells. They'd brought him down, eventually. They always did, but that's when things had changed. This time, the beating they gave him had been almost perfunctory. *Almost.* He was still going to feel like a tenderized piece of meat when the stun wore off and he could feel his limbs again. They usually focused their blows on areas where he was temporarily numb, leaving him in anticipation of the pain even before it began. It was one of their favorite petty torments, but they'd barely bothered this time. If he didn't know better, he might suspect they'd grown tired of punishing him, but years of abuse had torn away any hope he had of finding sympathy or mercy from his captors. Something else was going on, and change was never good. Not in this place. Still, he'd be more concerned if they hadn't beaten him at all. Kindness always came at a high price.

When the pain started, he rolled onto his stomach and pressed his face against the cold metal floor. His muscles twisted and writhed beneath his skin as neurons fired and nerve endings sang an aria of agony. He managed to shove a fist into his mouth to muffle any sound that might escape from between his gritted teeth. This cycle of pain—and then rebellion followed by more pain—was all he knew. And it would continue until the day he escaped from this hellish place or died trying.

He didn't want to die, though. Death would be an escape for him, but only for him. If he was killed, his brothers would still be imprisoned. Worse, one of them would have to take his place as the lead troublemaker. He suspected Mayhem would take over the job of pushing boundaries and making himself the target of any punishments as he continued to search for a way out.

He didn't want that role to fall to anyone else. Mayhem was strong and a good friend—one of the few he'd been allowed to see from time to time.

Once the fire in his muscles stopped, Rage rose to his feet, keeping his eyes half-closed to protect them from what came next. The lights came on, flooding the space with stark white light so bright it hurt his eyes. The scrawnies did it on purpose, the petty bastards.

He rose to his feet with a snarl of anger, flicking up two fingers on each hand in an obscene gesture he'd seen some of the low-level staff make when their superiors' backs were turned. Then he stretched out his aching muscles, making every motion fluid and easy despite the lingering pain of his beating. He would never show weakness when they were watching.

Never.

Once he'd finished his stretching routine, he moved over to the sink, letting the tepid water trickle into his cupped hands. He splashed it on his face to wash away any traces of blood. No glass was in the cell, but someone had bolted a plate of well-polished metal to the wall above the sink. He could see his reflection well enough to note the swelling of his cheek and the cut above one eyebrow that ran parallel to one of his brow markings. It would heal quickly. They always did.

Then he saw it. The real damage. *Fuck.* One of his horns was cracked. The part that curled around his ear and framed his jaw sported a new, ragged line longer than his thumb. He gathered more water into his hand and poured it over the damaged area. It was an instinctive action, one they all seemed to share. Each time one of them broke a horn or had one mutilated by their verexi captors, they all sought to soak the area in water. It worked too. Given enough moisture and time, the horn would heal itself. If there was another way to fix the damage, none of them knew what it was. Most of what they knew came from their captors, either through their instructional sessions or by watching the inane entertainment programs broadcast to their cells as a reward for good behavior. The rest was provided, in secret, by the single friend he had found in this hellish place—an android named Bysshe.

Bysshe was the unofficial liaison between the fa'rel and

their captors. The android did what he could to help them, somehow managing to keep that help a secret from the verexi while also finding ways to circumvent his programming. Rage didn't understand how that worked, really. Programs, machines, and technology were beyond him. It was enough to know that Bysshe existed. The how didn't matter.

Bysshe was an ally. He relayed messages between prisoners, helped in small ways, and tried to hide any transgressions to prevent or delay punishment from the verexi. He'd helped guide them when they were younger and still allowed to be together. Now that they were separated, Bysshe was the only connection they had to each other.

Rage's musings were interrupted by the soft tread of footsteps outside his cell door. The wall was solid, but he didn't need to see to know who was there. No one else moved like Bysshe. He was built to mimic a different species than the verexi. Shorter, stockier, and far less delicate, he'd taken blows that would have crippled or killed even the hardiest of the scrawnies.

"You are awake," Bysshe said in his flat, neutral voice.

"I am."

They fell into the familiar pattern. Bysshe recited his latest infractions in the stiff, formal language the verexi loved while Rage grunted at all the right times. While that went on, they had a very different conversation in the soft, subvocal undertones their jailors couldn't detect.

"How long will I be here this time?" Rage asked.

Bysshe answered after a long pause. "The rest of your life."

Rage felt a stab of foreboding, like an icy blade burrowing deep into his skin. "And how long will that be?"

Another silence followed, this one longer. Rage prowled the boundaries of his tiny cell as he waited for an answer.

"You are scheduled for termination."

The words hit him like another stun ray, numbing his limbs the same way they had during his failed escape attempt this morning. Rage went still, his hands flexing and claws extending without conscious thought.

Why now? He had been doing this for years—testing every part of this prison and looking for a way out. It was the only recreation he had. It was the focus of his life. Why were they punishing him *now*?

"When?"

Bysshe's voice went as dry as dust as he subvocalized, "I was not given that information."

In his normal voice, clipped and flat, he said, "Subject One. I have been instructed to inform you of your coming termination. You are advised to reflect on your life so far in order to prepare you for the next one. May the All-Seeing Ones have mercy on your soul."

With his next breath Bysshe added another message, this one spoken so softly Rage almost missed it. "I am sorry."

Rage froze, only a lifetime of practice keeping his expression neutral as he heard his fate. He wanted to throw back his head and howl in defiance. The dark fury that had led to his naming boiled up inside him, tinting his world red and urging him to tear this place down around the verexi's pointy ears. If he did that, though, he'd give away too much. They would be watching right now, observing everything he did, every breath, every motion. If he gave them what they wanted, they would *know*. If the verexi ever learned just how dangerous their experiments were, they'd kill him and all his brothers. He wouldn't let that happen.

He sheathed his claws and pushed out a breath through a throat that felt too tight. Then he drew himself up to his full height and nodded once before raising his eyes to the nearest camera. When he spoke, his words were twisted by a low snarl of pure fury. "I will be ready."

Bysshe scuffed his boot across the floor outside. To those listening, it would not mean anything, but to Rage, it was a warning. It meant be careful. Be ready.

Ready for what? He didn't know.

In his normal voice, he asked, "And the others? Do the scrawnies intend to punish them as well? They have done nothing wrong."

"You are the only one to be terminated." Bysshe's voice dropped into the subvocal tones no one else could hear. "For now."

Rage's anger rose up again, bitter and seething. They were *all* running out of time. The fa'rel had been created for a singular purpose—to become the verexi's army. Too frail to fight on their own, the scrawnies had been subjugated by most of the other races at one time or another. They were too weak to survive, yet somehow they had. It was more proof that the universe was a place of cruelty and fucking chaos.

He and his brothers were lab-born test subjects, and the tests had all resulted in failure. Despite the torturous training, experimental surgeries, and other hellish alterations to their physical and mental health, all the fa'rel still had free will. They would not obey orders blindly nor risk their lives because they were instructed to. They would never be the mindless killing machines their creators had envisioned... and that meant they were a liability. The day the risks outweighed the rewards, the scrawnies would terminate the project... and the fa'rel.

"I appreciate the information. I will be ready." Rage spoke the words aloud, but he knew Bysshe would understand the double meaning. He wasn't ready to die. He was ready to do whatever it took to escape this place... and somehow find a way to rescue the others.

2

MERCY

MERCY HATED THIS RUN. It wasn't the fact that it took her deep into the ass end of nowhere, though that was certainly inconvenient. It wasn't even the fact that she was in the verexi's space, a fact she tried not to dwell on too much. The alien race tended to treat humanity like something squelchy and unpleasant they found on the bottom of their shoe.

No, she hated this trip because the destination was her personal idea of hell.

The delivery run didn't even take her to an actual planet, for fuck's sake. The closest she came to whatever passed for civilization was a small, gray moon orbiting an empty planet on the edge of the system. The moon was as cold and barren as a crone's womb with nothing but the laboratory and landing pads nestled beneath an atmospheric dome.

If the place had a name, she'd never been given it. Just a mark on her star map, the journey represented a long, lonely venture into empty space with nothing to entertain her but a library of electronic books and vids and, of course, her collection of vibrators. She'd rather be doing one of a thousand other jobs, but this one paid the best, and she was in no position to walk away from steady income. The verexi were uptight assholes with egos as delicate as their constitutions, but their currency was one of the hardest in the galaxy. Every run brought her closer to her dream of leaving this life behind forever.

Mercy brought her ship down at the designated landing pad, following the directions sent to her nav-computer. She never spoke to anyone directly. All communication was written or relayed through the robots sent to unload the cargo. The closest she came to speaking to a living being were her chats with Bysshe, a human-made android whose presence was as strange and inexplicable as everything else about the place.

What did they do here? Whatever it was, it was clearly meant to be kept a secret. People with nothing to hide didn't set up shop so far from anything that it was actually

easier to bring in goods from outside the system than have them shipped from their homeworld. It was so desolate that damn near everything they needed had to be brought in from outside. Minimal water, no flora or fauna, and an atmosphere so thin they had to erect an atmospheric dome just to keep breathing. The whole place was gray—from the stones and the dirt to the sky above.

It gave her the creeps, which was yet another reason she hated this run. It was like delivering groceries to a graveyard... or something worse.

At the top of her "I don't want to know" list was the reason why this place required a steady supply of butchered animals. Not vat grown proteins but frozen slabs of actual meat filled her freezers every run. What the hell were they doing out here? That question wandered around her mind late at night, and the answers she came up with were fuel for her nightmares.

As usual, no one came out to greet her. She hadn't laid eyes on a single living being in the year she had been making this run. All she did was offload the freight and move on. Hells, it was pretty much all she did, period. This had been her life for as long as she'd been breathing, and before that her parents had done these long, lonely runs between the stars. They had eked out a living on the fringes of the civilized systems, surviving on scraps and pure human stubbornness. Forty years later, she was doing the same thing. Living the oh-so-glamorous life of a cargo pilot.

Mercy did her best to ignore her snarky inner dialogue, apart from making a note to up the caffeine content in her next cup of coffee. She opened the loading bay doors and tramped down the ramp to the concrete landing pad. The chill seeped into her bones in seconds, and a light mist swirled around her feet, making her hunch deeper into her jacket.

Weather. Ugh. This was why she didn't like planets. It was always too hot or too cold or too wet or drier than the ass crack of the star. Flying around in a tin can might not be the safest way to make a living, but at least she had complete control of her environment.

The usual fleet of robots scuttled out of the mist, heading her way. Bysshe would make his appearance soon to review the shipping manifest and oversee operations while the other bots offloaded the supplies. It never took long. It might take just over two standard weeks to get here, but she wouldn't be on the planet for more than twenty minutes or so. Then she'd travel two weeks back to something resembling civilization before she'd be on her next run. That's why this run paid so well. It had to, or no one would agree to do it. Nothing else was out this way thus no chance to add other clients to the list. It was also why no one else wanted this long, solitary run and usually left as quickly as they could. Mercy had seen the advantages right away and had never complained. Well, not too much, and never where she could be heard.

As usual, most of the bots went straight for the cargo hatch, scanning barcodes and then whisking the containers away. She had no idea where they went, and she did her best to ignore the part of her that was curious about what went on here. If she wanted to keep her job, she'd best not ask questions.

Bysshe showed up a few seconds later, striding through the surge of bots that scuttled and buzzed around his legs. He was more or less human looking, with a masculine build and generic features. He was also pale blue and hairless with eyes so dark she couldn't tell if they were black or deep blue. She'd seen androids before, but never up close and never outside the pitiful handful of human settlements still in existence.

"Captain Johnson. It is always a pleasure to see you," Bysshe greeted her. She had no idea what language he spoke, though she assumed it was verexi. Her translator was programmed with all known languages and dialects, so all she heard was clear, straightforward Terran.

"Hello, Bysshe. Nice to see you, too." She tapped her wrist unit and sent the manifest to the android. "They shorted you two crates of gestak, but I managed to snag a few extra boxes of targesh to make up for it."

The android nodded. "Thank you."

A note popped up on her wrist unit from Bysshe. This was how they communicated when he didn't want the other bots to overhear their conversation. *"And my personal order?"*

"Inside crate forty-seven. Bottom left," she typed back.

The android flashed her a shadow of a smile—the only acknowledgment she'd get, which was fine. She wasn't looking for thanks. She was only after the fund transfer that would appear before she left this miserable rock. She had no idea what the android needed medical supplies for or how a possession like him had access to currency at all, but these little side deals paid too well to ask any questions.

They passed the time with small talk, which wasn't her favorite pastime, but after two weeks alone, the android made surprisingly good company. The cargo bays and freezers were almost empty when Bysshe sent another message to her wrist unit.

"This base is being decommissioned soon. I have seen the paperwork. When that happens, your contract will be terminated. I have not been instructed to tell you this yet, but I thought you should be aware of the coming change."

Well, *shit*. That threw a black hole into the middle of her fucking flight plan.

"Thank you for the early warning. Appreciate it. How long do I have?" she typed back.

Bysshe checked the cargo bay for potential eavesdroppers, but the space was empty. The last of the bots had scuttled off with a box clamped to the top of its carapace, so they were alone.

This time, he spoke, though very softly. "Another run. Maybe two."

She didn't bother to hide her dismay. The android would know she was agitated just by her heart rate and body language. There was no way to hide the truth from a machine like him. Hell, Bysshe wasn't actually a *him* at all. Her mind just assigned that pronoun because it suited his appearance.

"Not sure what I'm going to miss most—the money or your smiling face each time I visit," she joked.

Bysshe cocked his head in momentary confusion as his neural matrix attempted to decipher her joke. "Ah. Humor. I see," he said and then gave her his best attempt at a smile. "If you are interested, I have another deal to offer you. This one should mitigate the financial pain you will experience when this contract ends."

"What is it?" she asked warily.

"You have an empty hold. I have cargo I'd like transported."

"I don't move drugs, weapons, or slaves," she warned him.

"The package is none of those things. However, it is a time-sensitive offer. It would have to be loaded today. Immediately, in fact. And if discovered, your contract could be terminated early. There is some... risk."

Risk was a way of life out here. If the reward was high enough, she'd be a fool to say no. "How much?"

The android named a sum so high she thought she'd misheard him. "Say that again?"

He repeated the offer and then continued, "Payment will be made by the usual means. I assume you will want it up front?"

"That would be preferable." She held out her hand to him, pleased to note her fingers weren't shaking. "We have a deal."

"Then this will likely be the last time you and I will meet." He took her hand, shook it, and then gave her a stiff little bow. "It has been a pleasure, Captain Johnson."

That was it? That couldn't be it. "Wait. What about the cargo? How is it getting on board? Where do you want me to deliver it?"

"It will arrive shortly. Once it's aboard, I recommend a rapid departure. The rest of the instructions will be with the package. I trust you to do what is needed to ensure a safe journey."

"Of course. Safety is my middle name."

The android's eyes widened, and she hurriedly added, "Not really. That was another joke."

Bad enough her parents had named her Mercy, a thing she'd seen very little of in her life. Mercy Safety would have been an open invitation to the universe to heap abuse down on her head until it buried her.

"I'll start prepping the ship for launch. How will I know when your package arrives?"

Bysshe's eyes crinkled slightly at the corners and his next words were spoken in a tone so dry she had a sudden urge to pour herself a drink. "Don't worry, Captain. You'll know."

Oh no, that wasn't ominous. Not at all. What in the nine hells had she gotten herself into this time? Whatever it was, she already regretted it. A smart woman would fire up the engines and get out of here as fast as possible. But a smart woman wouldn't have agreed to a deal without knowing more about it. This ship and her integrity were about all she had worth anything, and she wasn't going to lose either one.

She'd stay, take on this mysterious cargo, and deal with the consequences later. What was the worst that could happen?

3

RAGE

WHEN THE DOOR to his cell unlocked Rage froze, ignoring his first instinct—to run. It could be a trap. It had to be unless *this* was the sign Bysshe had told him to be ready for. Was it?

On the heels of those questions came another one. What did it matter? Death was already coming for him. Dying in a trap meant he had a chance to take some of his tormentors with him. That would have to be enough.

The corridor outside his door was empty. No sounds. No scents. Not even the usual hum of the power lines that snaked through the walls. Someone had cut power to this area. No power meant no automated security measures or cameras. No one could see him right now.

He ran.

Enough light was leaking in beneath the doors and cracks to let him find his way through the maze of corridors. He'd mapped most of them in his years here, committing them to memory one step at a time. He couldn't reach his brothers from here. They were behind too many walls and doors that would not open without key cards he had never managed to keep for more than a few minutes.

Guilt tore through him as understanding dawned. He couldn't free them. He'd have to leave his brothers here. It felt like cowardice... but it was the only chance he had. He was no good to them dead.

Rage ran on, his nerves singing as he raced ever closer to the main doors. Unlike the verexi, he could survive in the thin atmosphere beyond the dome. He'd managed to get that far twice before. Once, he'd even stayed free for an entire night. None of the others had ever gotten that far. Not that he had heard.

He hit the doors at full speed, flinging them open with enough force to tear the hinges away.

The barrage of stunner fire he'd braced himself for didn't come. No one shouted. No alarms erupted in an ear-piercing clamor. He tore across the open space between the buildings, looking for the shortest path to the edge of the dome. Then he saw something else.

A ship.

At least, that's what it looked like. He'd only seen images of one until now. It was a hulking pile of metal reeking of chemicals that stung his nose, and the noise it made was enough to make him clap his hands over his ears. Any other day, he'd have run as far from it as he could but not today. Not when he could see the mark Bysshe had left on the ramp that extended down to the ground.

It was the symbol for "safety" along with an arrow that pointed inside the ship. The scrawnies' vision was limited to only a few colors, and the symbol was painted in a hue they couldn't see. Probably placed there by one of the worker bots based on the tracks he could see in the paint.

This was better than running off into the barren wasteland beyond the domes to hide. A ship meant a chance to escape forever.

I'm sorry, my brothers. I will find a way to free you someday. The unspoken promise rankled, like a sliver under his skin. This wasn't how he'd envisioned this moment, but it would have to do.

His best chance to save the others was to get on that ship and enlist whatever help he found inside. Who was on board? Why were they out here? And why in the name of the All-Seeing Ones would Bysshe trust them?

The only way to learn the answers was to get to that vessel and escape.

Fifty strides to the ramp. Thirty. Twenty. The roar of the engines intensified until he could feel the ground tremble beneath his bare feet. He was going to make it!

The first shot scored the tarmac to his left, an eye-searing bolt of angry orange light that tore into the solid surface like a claw ripping through flesh. He snarled in defiance, changing directions every two strides to avoid getting hit. Those weren't stunner bolts. Those were something else… and he wanted no part of them.

He reached the ramp and hurtled up it, his head down and eyes fixed on the far wall of the cargo area. The ramp lifted while he was still on it, the sudden change making him stagger. That action saved his life.

A bolt grazed the top of his shoulder, plowing through the skin and a bit of the muscle. He howled in pain but kept moving, tumbling down the ramp and into the cargo bay.

He fell, the shock of impact sending another bolt of raw agony through his body. The floor shook beneath him and then a giant hand settled on his back and pressed down until he thought his ribs would shatter. Somewhere in the distance, he heard a voice unlike any other he'd heard before. It was light and lilting, the familiar verexi language elevated into something almost appealing. All it said was, "Welcome aboard the *Timeless Blue*. Hang on. I'm sending a med-droid. We'll get you to the med-bay once we're in the clear of these assholes."

Rage grinned. Whoever was flying this thing didn't think much of the verexi. That had to be a good sign. Closing his eyes, he offered up a silent thank you to Bysshe. He didn't know how the android had done it, but Rage owed him his life. Someday, he'd find a way to repay the favor.

4

MERCY

SOMEDAY, she'd learn not to agree to things without reading the fucking fine print. Her "package" was a prisoner, and judging by the firepower aimed at him and her ship, the verexi weren't happy he'd escaped.

Mercy turned off the ship-wide comm system and threw her hands in the air. "Fuck!"

If she ever saw that blue-balled android again, she'd have a few things to say to him. If she didn't skip the talking part and shoot him on sight.

"What the hells am I going to do with an escaped prisoner?" she muttered to herself as she prepped the ship's star drive. Protocol stated she couldn't activate them until she reached a minimum safe distance from all gravity wells. However, protocol could take a swan dive into the nearest black hole this time. The moment the *Blue* was ready to transit to hyperspace, she was red-lining the engines all the way back to her home port in the Gilvery Cluster.

A continuous stream of messages from the installation below flooded her comms. Her console pinged each time a new one arrived, and the noise was not helping her stress level.

"Fuck off already!" she snapped at the console. "The time for pleasantries went out the airlock the second you assholes opened fire on my ship."

The least they could have done was send a message warning her. It wouldn't change anything, but they didn't know that. For all they knew, she was an innocent bystander in all this fuckery. Hells, she didn't even know what her package was until he'd charged for her ship in all his bare-assed glory. She'd seen a lot of strange things over the years, but a naked jailbreak was one for the books.

His lack of clothing had stopped her from breaking her word and taking off before the prisoner reached her. Any man desperate or brave enough to sprint buck naked through a hail of enemy fire was worthy of her admiration... and it had nothing to do with the eyeful of hard muscle and broad shoulders that appeared on her viewscreen while she watched his approach. Nothing at all. Nope.

Of course, she couldn't be sure that her new passenger was male. Her "package" definitely had a nice package, but alien biology was a tricky thing to judge, especially when dealing with a new species... and whatever her package was, he was definitely *not* human.

As far as she was concerned, that was a point in his favor.

His favorability rating climbed again when she took her eyes off the monitors long enough to check the balance of her account. Jackpot! Bysshe had held up his side of the deal. In fact, she now had a hells of a lot more in her account than she'd expected. Bysshe had transferred her enough money to ensure she'd never go hungry again. That told her just how much her passenger's life meant to the odd android. He was giving her every reason to protect and deliver the package safely.

"I'll take care of it," she said aloud, the words solidifying her decision. She'd do this for Bysshe, not because of the money but because someone in this fucked up universe needed help and had trusted her enough to ask for it. That wasn't an honor she could walk away from, which meant she had to deal with big, blond, and well-built just as soon as she was sure no one was following them or trying to blow them out of the sky.

Being followed wasn't likely, though. Mercy had never seen another ship in this sector, never mind on the moon itself. Only two landing pads were located anywhere near what she assumed was the warehouse, with no hangars or bays for any kind of aircraft. Whatever the installation's purpose, no one was supposed to leave. Which meant whoever was sitting in her cargo bay right now wasn't supposed to leave, either. Not a comforting thought, but she only had the bandwidth for one crisis at a time. Right now, she was more worried about being shot at.

The lunar installation may not have ships, but it did have guns. According to her scans, they had an entire battery of ship-killers set up on the perimeter of the domes, enough to keep even the most desperate of raiders at bay. It made sense they'd be armed. They were on their own out here with no military support. It was exactly the kind of tempting target pirates looking to steal anything they could get their hands, claws, or pseudopods on loved best.

As if reading her thoughts, the ship's systems erupted

with warnings as multiple missiles launched from the surface. She checked her ship's progress and was surprised to notice they were almost out of range already. The weaponry must take time to power up, which meant if she could out fly this first barrage, they'd be free and clear.

She flipped on the ship-wide channel and relayed a terse warning to her passenger. "You'd better hang on to something back there. This ride is about to get bumpy."

She double checked her safety harness, turned off the gravity in the cockpit, and took manual control. It was time to do some fancy flying.

Her hands flew over the controls as she put the *Blue* into a series of pitches and turns that stressed the old girl to her limits. Mercy patted the console gently. "Sorry, girl. You stay in one piece for this run and I promise I'll make it up to you. How does a new plasma matrix and a fresh coat of nano-particulate paint sound?"

In all the years she'd talked to the ship this way, it had never answered her. So when a strange voice came from behind her, she nearly levitated out of her seat.

"Why offer bribes to a machine?"

"Fucking hell!" she yelled, not taking her eyes off the monitors. "Didn't anyone tell you to never distract the pilot when she's flying the fucking ship? Especially not when we're under attack?"

She spun the ship ninety degrees to the left, a lifetime of space travel allowing her to maintain her equilibrium. She expected the land-dwelling alien to bounce off the walls like a ping-pong ball in freefall, but that didn't happen.

All she heard were several odd, metallic pings. When

she looked back, she found her new passenger had slammed clawed hands into the bulkhead on either side of the cockpit. He had braced himself there in a show of strength that would be more impressive if he hadn't just punched holes in the walls of her ship.

"You break it, you buy it," she muttered and turned her attention back to the monitors. The last of the missiles were ahead of them now, and the ship's automated defenses took them out before they could reorient on their target.

As the last of the red blips vanished from her screen, she exhaled and reactivated gravity. Then she righted the ship and activated the star drive before slumping back in her chair.

"We're clear," she said and patted the console again. "Good job, girl."

"The ship did nothing you didn't tell it to do. Why praise it? You are the pilot. You should congratulate yourself."

Mercy spun around to face her passenger. That's when two things struck her. One, he was huge. The cockpit was originally laid out for a three-man crew, but he took up all the available space. Two, he was still naked—delightfully, distractingly naked, apart from the field dressing her medical bot had applied to his injured shoulder. Her gaze drifted down his body, taking in every detail. Dark blond hair. Golden skin... or was that fur? Big amber eyes surrounded by a ring of black, and dark marks over his eyes that vanished into his hair, and horns.

Does that mean he's horny? Some twisted part of her mind whispered to the rest of her.

Big horns, big feet, big... Another part observed.

Stop that. She was losing her mind over a male. What in the hells was wrong with her? Granted, he was an impressive specimen of prime manhood. Malehood? Whatever, he was young enough to be all toned muscle and unwrinkled skin.

He was definitely pretty, but he was also a stranger, an escaped prisoner, and a whole lot of trouble wrapped up in a tempting package.

She unbuckled her harness and raised her head so she could look him in the eyes. He'd retracted his claws and lowered his arms to his sides in a stance that reminded her of a soldier at parade rest.

"Welcome aboard. You got a name?" They'd already spoken, so despite the fact she didn't recognize his species, he spoke one of the known languages. If he didn't, her translator wouldn't have worked.

He stared at her for a few seconds before answering. "I am Rage."

She bit her lip to hold back a bout of involuntary laughter and managed a polite nod instead. Translators were finicky things, and for all she knew in his language his name might mean something totally innocuous.

She rose. "I'm Mercy. Let's get you to the med-bay and get your shoulder fixed. Then you and I need to have a chat about why you're on my ship and what the fuck I'm going to do with you now that you're here."

5

RAGE

THIS WAS ALL VERY STRANGE. This female was the first person he'd ever met who wasn't verexi. In fact, she was the first female he'd ever met of any species, other than the pleasure bots the verexi had provided to the fa'rel once they reached sexual maturity.

She wasn't already versed in every detail of his life, and she hadn't called him by the only name he'd known until he'd chosen one for himself. He wasn't Subject One anymore. He was Rage, and he was *free*.

But his brothers weren't. Not yet. He would not leave without them. "We have to go back."

The female was tiny and delicate compared to him, but her laugh carried a tone of command. "No."

He snarled and bared his fangs at her, an act that used to send the verexi scuttling for the nearest exit. "You will do as I say."

He expected her to flinch away from him, to quail or scream with fear. She didn't. This little female did none of those things. She rose to her full height, locked her dark eyes on his, and laughed louder. "Don't even try to pull that macho, chest thumping bullshit with me. I don't know what you are or what you did to get sent to that hellscape, but this is my ship, and I give the orders here."

Her confidence intrigued him as did the subtle lines that marked her face, especially around the corners of her eyes. He was about to ask her what they were, but before he could, she stepped into his space and poked him in the center of his chest. "I'm the boss. We clear on that?"

He raised his hand to bat hers away but then froze as his annoyance was replaced by something else. The moment of contact became a moment of connection. He forgot about her challenge and the way her confidence called to him. All thought of his brothers and even the vague pain in his shoulder vanished. All he could think of was *her*.

Need thrummed through him, primal and more powerful than anything he had ever experienced before. Not even the raw need that tore at him all through his transition to adulthood had been this strong—back in the days when his captors had brought in machines with pleasing shapes and soft voices that he could use to take the edge off his sexual hunger.

He had used them and learned from them, rutting with them for hours until the worst had passed. He'd found pleasure with them as well as the blissful sleep of exhaustion, but he'd never been satisfied.

This felt different. He could feel it in his balls and the slow, steady throbbing of his cock.

He didn't understand why, but right now he didn't care. She wasn't the same race as him. She wasn't submissive or sensual the way the pleasure bots had been, but none of that mattered. He craved her... and he would have her.

He captured her small hand in his and then took a moment to drink her in. Her skin was darker than his, and her eyes were brown with a cluster of gold around her iris. She had hair the color of the night sky he'd seen during his brief moments of freedom, deep black with twinkling hints of star-lit silver here and there.

He reached up to touch her cheek, careful to keep his claws retracted as he ran his fingertips over her skin and to her ear. Her hair was shorn almost to the scalp at the sides but rose up at the center into a line of intricate twists that followed the curve of her skull.

She had no horns and no markings he could see, but to him, she was beautiful. In fact, she was perfect.

"You belong to me."

Her lips parted on a startled gasp and her scent strengthened, filling his lungs with the promise of... he didn't know what, but he wanted more of it. What he got instead was a blow to the stomach from one of her tiny hands. It tickled.

"No." Her tone held more warning than the punch she'd thrown. No one dared to speak to him that way. He ruled over the rest of his clan, and the verexi might be his captors, but even they were afraid of him... as they should be.

This female was not. In fact, she was defying him.

"Yes," he retorted. "I do not understand it, but that doesn't change things. You are mine." He chuffed out a laugh as her lip curled up in an adorable little snarl.

"I don't fucking think so." This time, her attempt to

strike him wasn't a surprise. Her chosen target was. Her hand shot down, slender fingers clamping down on his balls and squeezing hard enough to get his full attention.

He caught her by the wrist but made no attempt to tear her hand away. The pain was nothing compared to the pleasure of her touch.

"You're wrong. You are mine." He grinned. "The only Mercy I have ever known."

"Not the time for puns, big guy. You need to back off before I do some permanent damage to your equipment." For a brief moment, her grip relaxed, and she looked almost regretful. "That would be unfair to whatever female decides to accept your heavy-handed attempts to bed her."

"There will be no others. Only you." He had no idea where that thought had come from, but the idea of sampling the pleasure of any other female didn't appeal to him anymore. After years of dreaming about what he'd do with his freedom—indulging in every vice and experience he could find—reality had presented him with another option. He didn't want every pleasure anymore. He wanted her. *Now.*

And for the first time in his life, he was free to take what he wanted.

He crowded her into the nearest bulkhead, not stopping until she was pressed between the metal and his bare skin.

"You wear too many pieces of fabric. They annoy me. Remove them."

She snorted and glared up at him, her delicate fingers tightening around his scrotum until the pain eclipsed the pleasure. "Your attitude is annoying me. Remove *it.*"

He grinned despite the discomfort, flashing his fangs. "I

cannot. It is part of me." He bowed his head until his lips were only a hairsbreadth away from hers. "As are you."

"See? That's annoying." Her free hand moved, and before he knew what was happening the little female had a blade against his throat. "Stop it. Now."

Admiration and lust tore through him, sending more blood rushing to his cock. He was harder than he'd ever been in his life. "I can't. You are..." he shook his head, words failing him.

"If the next word out of your mouth is 'mine,' I will have to stab you on principle."

He laughed and then moved with all the speed he possessed, snatching the weapon away from her and knocking her other hand off his balls before she did something they would both regret.

He didn't move far from her, just enough to disarm her without giving her the freedom to flee. They'd have time for that later. He would chase her around this ship, taking her against every surface until she accepted what he already knew... she was his. He was not good with words. He'd had little chance to communicate with anyone other than his captors and his clan. He would have to show her instead.

She yelled in frustration and threw herself at him, her fingers curved into claws. Instead of deflecting her attack, he pulled her in close, ignoring the sting of her nails as he hauled her up against his chest.

She hissed and struggled, every motion arousing him even more. Then instinct kicked in and he did something he'd never done before. He bowed his head and crushed her mouth with his.

6
MERCY

THE ONLY THING more annoying than an arrogant, domineering man was an arrogant, domineering, sexy as hell *alien* male. Worse, somewhere around the time she'd tried to lay down the law with her new passenger, her libido had taken control and overridden her small but treasured stash of common sense. She should be escorting his naked, annoying ass to the nearest cabin and locking him inside it for the duration of the voyage. Instead, all she wanted to do was climb him like he was the world's biggest sundae and declare herself the cherry on top.

He'd looked good before, but once she laid her hand on the silky hair that covered his hard-as-steel chest, she'd lost her damned mind and hadn't managed to get it back yet.

Then he'd kissed her, and she'd stopped trying to reclaim even a modicum of sanity. If this was the moment her mind snapped, she was willing to go mad... just as long as he didn't stop what he was doing.

She'd appreciated his body the moment she'd seen it on camera, but now she'd viewed it up close and oh so personally, she couldn't get enough of him. Soft fur covered hard muscle, and sharp canines grazed her lips as he plundered her mouth with more hunger than style. It reminded her of the first kisses she'd ever had—eager, sometimes clumsy, and pulsing with the fire of youth.

His passion was like that but more, as raw and brutal as he was. And holy nukes and novas, she liked it. Muscle and sinew flowed beneath his skin like steel under velvet. Whoever he was. Whatever he was, he was danger and power personified. But a little voice whispered that he was no threat to her.

That little voice had to belong to the part of her that had lost the fucking plot. She didn't do random hookups anymore. Especially with impossibly hot young men with bodies built for all sorts of sins.

Tiny stings pierced her awareness. But desire had befuddled her reflexes so she didn't move until it was too late. He tore through her clothes with his claws, letting the shredded fabric fall away. She was naked in a matter of seconds.

"Hey! You're going to pay for replacements."

"I have no money," he said, his words almost lost beneath a new noise that sounded oddly like...

"Are you *purring*?" she asked.

"I am... I don't know what it's called. I make this noise when I am well-pleasured." He grinned at her. "Or about to be. How much pleasure will it take for you to consider the debt paid off?"

Holy hells. Had he just offered to pay her off in orgasms? That was the most offensively arrogant offer she'd ever had. And the most tempting.

She cast about for some logical reason for her sudden onset of sexual insanity. *Pheromones.* That was a thing. Right? That had to be what was going on here because she was on the verge of naming a price that was purely carnal.

He folded her against his chest, the rumbling purr growing deeper and making her throb in places that had never so much as quivered before. He stroked her bare skin, exploring her with gentle fingers as his claws grazed lightly over aroused flesh.

She rose on her toes, hands moving from his chest to his shoulders and then up into the long, golden hair of his head. It was thicker than she expected, more like a mane than human hair... but of course, Rage wasn't human, a fact that grew more obvious every second.

His scent was a blend of musk and spices and his lips tasted like candied sin—hot, sweet, and addictive. His hands slid down her back, palming the cheeks of her ass as he pressed the hard bar of his cock against her body. She could swear he felt bigger now, and he had raised ridges she hadn't noticed before.

When he lifted her off the deck, she went willingly, too far gone with whatever madness this was to resist. She wrapped her legs around his hips, his tongue spearing into her mouth as he pinned her against the bulkhead. This was more than lust or the need to let off some steam after her adrenaline-fueled escape. She should be afraid of just how out of control she was, but she wasn't. The thought skittered and skipped around the edges of her mind as most of her gray matter turned to sizzling mush.

Small details grew, taking up all of her awareness. The

chill of the metal wall against her fevered skin made her arch away, so she rubbed up against him instead.

Silky fur caressed her nipples, sending shards of pleasure zinging through her body and adding more fuel to the fires already burning. He lifted her higher and then brought her down slowly, positioning the thick head of his cock against the folds of her pussy. She was wet and ready for him even though he'd barely touched her. How was this happening?

Pheromones. That little voice whispered. Oh, right.

He held them like that for what felt like forever until she realized he was waiting for her permission. Her lips quirked up at that.

She was still in control, sort of. That was good enough. "Yes," the single word was torn from her throat to hum against his lips.

His purr deepened, but he stayed frustratingly still. She wriggled against him, tightening her legs and gripping his shoulders, careful to avoid his injury while still trying to take what she needed. "I said yes already."

"Admit you are mine," he demanded.

"No." Denying the arrogant young buck took more willpower than she'd ever admit to anyone, but she managed it. This time.

Rage rocked his hips, sliding those intriguing cock ridges across her clit. *Fuck,* that felt good. Too good. Her will weakened and then buckled faster than a bad hull repair in a vacuum. "Yours," she bit out the word like it was poisonous, raising one hand to grip the horn that curled beside his jaw. He stiffened, every muscle tensing for a moment before exhaling with a snarl that melted what was left of her mind.

"Do you want me, Rage?" she asked softly.

He stared into her eyes, his amber ones almost glowing with desire. "Yes."

"Then I think *you* belong to *me*." It was official. She'd lost her damn mind. The last thing she wanted was to lay claim to this sexy, snarly, arrogant furball. But she already had... and she couldn't bring herself to regret it.

"Yes." Rage's answer surprised her.

Her brain—or at least what was left of it—fell out of orbit to crash on the surface of the planet what-the-fuck. "What?"

"You are mine, and I am yours." He surged upward, filling her completely with one bruising, powerful thrust.

She caught hold of his horn with her free hand, gripping it like a handle and pulling his mouth to hers. "Ditto," she whispered as she kissed him. She could think of a thousand reasons this couldn't last, but fuck it. She'd enjoy the moment and deal with the consequences later.

7

***

RAGE

He DIDN'T KNOW what was most appealing about the curvy little spitfire—her passion, her confidence, or the fact she wasn't afraid of him. He didn't spend any time working it out, either. He had better things to do. He had a female to pleasure. *His* female.

Freedom could be lost too easily for him to let these moments slip away. However long he had, he intended to spend it all buried balls deep inside her. Starting now.

He pushed into her body, not stopping until he was sheathed in the slick heat of her cunt. She was nothing like the pleasure bots his captors had provided. She was tight, and hot, and the sounds of their mutual pleasure filled the air like music.

She moaned and quivered around him, her slender fingers still curled around his horn. Her touch undid him, every caress of her hands threatening to shatter what was left of his mind.

He withdrew from her, letting the ridges of his cock slide along her inner walls as they flexed around him. He pulled back until only the tip of him still rested inside her, pausing just long enough to tease them both.

"Don't make love to me," she whispered. "Fuck me. I won't break, Rage."

He didn't understand what the first part meant, but the rest was clear enough. After a lifetime of resisting every order he'd been given, this was one he was happy to follow. He dropped the last chains binding his control and gave her everything she'd asked for—everything and more.

He claimed her body with his, losing himself in the heat of their combined passions. She was freedom made flesh, and he would never let her go. "Mine," he snarled the single word against her lips before kissing her deeply, his tongue dancing to the same driving beat as his cock as they mated.

Her hands slipped from his horns to his shoulders, her tiny nails curling into his fur. Her teeth sank into his lower lip hard enough to draw blood, the taste of it spreading over his tongue and hers.

He raised her higher, changing the angle between their bodies to increase the friction between them. Something was happening. He didn't know what it was, but he could feel it building. It simmered in his blood like a fever only she could cure.

The rhythm between them changed, becoming erratic as he drove into her. Each thrust pinned her to the metal wall of the ship. She was so small he could be hurting her, but all he heard were her cries of pleasure with no hint of pain or fear.

He tore his mouth from hers and then threw back his head to roar at the stars. She joined him in that moment, raising her voice to echo his as his cock swelled and his balls tightened. Pleasure uncoiled deep in his groin, tearing through him and taking him far beyond anything he'd ever known before.

The ridges on his cock flared, expanding until they were locked together as he emptied himself inside her, branding her with his essence.

She came apart around him, her inner walls gripping his cock and milking every bit of seed from his balls. They stayed like that, both of them lost in what felt like unending ecstasy.

She quivered and writhed against him, held fast in his arms until the storm passed. He sank to the floor with her cradled against him, her legs still wrapped around his waist. Her lips feathered soft, breathy kisses on his cheeks.

He lifted his head to speak but stopped when a new sensation blazed into his awareness. The skin on his chest tingled and then burned. His lips curled back into a snarl, but before he could do anything else the pain faded away.

He looked down at his chest, expecting to see blood or a wound of some kind. All he saw were black marks across his fur that hadn't been there until now.

"Scars?" Mercy asked, her voice almost as soft as her touch when she traced the lines. "Like claw marks?"

She was right. He leaned back, giving himself enough room to move. He raised a hand, extended his claws, and held them over the new markings. They were a perfect match.

Mercy placed one hand over his, splaying her fingers widely enough to match the strange new lines. She drew her fingers down the lines, starting at his shoulders and crossing over his chest in an X. "What did this? Why?"

"I don't know." He shrugged. "I stopped asking that question a long time ago. The verexi never gave us any answers."

"Us?" The little female's tone had lost its sultry softness. "More of you are back there?"

"My brothers."

Her lips thinned, and she gave him a tight nod. "That's why you wanted to go back."

"Yes. Can we go back now?"

She shook her head. "We got lucky last time. We were nearly out of range before they got their guns primed to fire. If we go back, they'll blow us to the nine hells long before we can land. This is a freighter, not a warship."

He scowled and uttered a low growl of frustration. "Where can I find warships?"

Mercy snorted. "A sane person wouldn't ask that question. Most of us try to avoid them at all costs."

He slammed his fist into the floor, denting it. "Then how do I free my clan?"

He didn't recognize the look in her eyes at first. He'd never seen it on another being, except in the videos the verexi allowed them to view sometimes. It was *pity*.

That wasn't acceptable.

"No." He lifted her up and set her down beside him on the chill floor. "We have to free them. I am the eldest. I swore…"

She raised a hand and pressed a finger to his lips. "Shush. You won't save anyone if you're dead. I understand promises. Made a few myself. Kept them, too. Mostly. Take it from someone older and theoretically wiser than you. Some promises take longer to keep." She quirked a dark brow. "And that is the last time I will ever admit to being older than you. Bring it up again and I'll make you pay for it."

"I don't know how much time they have." Frustration still had him in a stranglehold, but he recognized her attempt to calm him with jokes. Her age didn't matter. She was his Mercy. That was the only truth he cared about. She had to help him free the others.

"Bysshe knew. He told me that my contract would end soon because that place, whatever it is, was shutting down."

He chewed on each word before spitting it out. "It's a verexi laboratory. They made us. Experimented on us. If they are shutting down that place, the others..." The dent in the floor deepened as he slammed his fist down several more times. They'd kill them. Or move them so he'd never find them again. He wouldn't let that happen. He would not lose them. They were all he had.

Mercy caught his fist in her hands. "Beating up my deck isn't going to change anything. We'll figure this out. Whatever they're planning can't happen right away. There are no ships in the area. We have a little time."

We. No one besides his brothers had ever used that word. "You will help?"

She shot him a frustrated look. "Of course I'll help. Bysshe paid me very well to get you off that planet. More than he promised me, in fact. I assume that's because the job isn't done yet. He knew you'd need the money. That is one sneaky android."

He reared back, stung. "You think of this as a job?" This time, he didn't just hit the deck plate. He punched his claws through it.

Her brows scrunched together, creasing her dark skin around her stormy eyes. Then the storm cleared and she shook her head softly. "Honestly? I have no idea what this is. You... this... this is as weird for me as it is for you. I don't normally sleep with my passengers. Hell, I don't normally have passengers, period. But... she raised her arms. Black marks, smaller versions of the ones on his chest had appeared on her forearms. They started at her palms and wrapped around to cross over the top of her wrists.

"Whatever the fuck is happening, it appears we're in it together."

"What is that? What does it mean?" he asked.

Mercy laughed. "Fuck if I know. Humans don't spontaneously manifest random markings. So whatever this is, I'm blaming you for it."

She got to her feet, leaving the pile of shredded fabric on the floor. Her curvy body distracted him, and he wanted nothing more than to pull her back into his arms and make her scream his name again. But that would have to wait... for a little while.

8

MERCY

SHE HADN'T NOTICED when the marks appeared on her wrists. Her senses had been on overload, and her body was still quivering with orgasmic aftershocks. She was having a hard time thinking clearly, and the last thing she'd considered doing was checking herself for randomly appearing marks. They were hard to see against her dark skin, but they were there, and she took that as a sign that somehow, someway, her destiny was tied to Rage's.

This was not what she'd been expecting when she'd rolled out of her bunk this morning. Breakfast, a delivery, and then nothing to do until she got back to civilization. Instead, she'd gotten a heaping serving of trouble with a side order of sexy alien. The universe had clearly been drunk when it had come up with this plan, and she was certain she was going to need a few drinks and some time before she came to terms with it all. He was young, brash, and unbridled, a reminder of all the things she'd been once.

That was a long time ago, though. She'd been alone so long, toiling to pay off her parents' debts as well as her own.

They'd died long since, but she hadn't given up. She'd pushed on, day after day, grinding through the years until she'd managed to free herself. And now, apparently, she had a new agenda... and a partner. Holy hells. A partner. A lover. A Rage.

Something kindled in her heart at the thought. A fire she'd thought had gone out sparked to life again. She had to be crazy, but what the hells. What did she have to lose?

First things first, though. They needed a plan if they were going to free the rest of her alien's clan. Too bad she had no idea how the hells to do it. They had no army, no weapons, and nothing to go on apart from a supernova's worth of physical chemistry between her and a lab experiment gone rogue.

Rage got to his feet, looming over her like a predator ready to chow down on his next meal. "I don't know what these marks are, so you can't blame me for them. They bind us somehow. You are mine now, and I am yours." He crossed his arms over his chest and then drew his claw over the marks in a slashing motion.

"What, like fate? Divine intervention?" She shook her head and made a negating motion with both hands. "I don't believe in any of that. We're born. We die. The rest is just random chance and zaktar shit."

"I was born in a lab. The only freedom I have ever known were fleeting moments when I broke out, but I didn't have anywhere to go. No real escape. Not until today." He thumped his big hand against his even bigger chest and grinned. It was a primal expression—fierce, dangerous, and seriously sexy. "We will make our own destiny."

She should have laughed at the arrogance of that

statement. Or run. Running would have been smart. Instead, she moved into his space, wrapping her arms around his waist with her head on his broad chest. "Yeah, we will. You and me. Together."

It was the craziest thing she'd ever said, and she meant every word. She was so fucked.

The first seeds of an idea sprouted while she was trying to keep Rage still. The med-bay's system was regenerating his shoulder wound, but a lifetime of abuse had left the big growly guy with trust issues the size of a planet. She had to explain everything the system was going to do before he would allow it, and then she had to remind him to hold still during the procedure.

In the end, she opted to distract him. He might not be human, but males were all the same. If you petted the right parts, their brains stopped working. She parted his thighs and claimed a spot between them as he watched her with his dazzling amber eyes.

"What?" he growled at her.

"This." She tried to growl back, gave up, and wrapped her fingers around the impressive length of his cock. He hardened quickly, the air of the med-bay filling with the low rumble of his purr as she stroked him. His cock twitched in her hand, his eyes partially closed now and his head tipped back in pure male enjoyment as she learned what he liked.

By the time the med-system was finished, Rage was only thinking about one thing and she was happy to oblige.

He pulled her in close, kissing her hard. Then he was

on his feet, spinning them both around so she was bent over the bed he'd been on only seconds before.

Before she could protest, he had his hand between her thighs, already working two thick fingers into her pussy while using another to stroke her clit. She whimpered, gripped the bed, and held on as the sound of his purr grew louder, punctuated with the occasional snarl.

It was the sexiest thing she'd ever heard.

He pressed her thighs apart, sinking to his knees behind her. When his mouth latched on to her clit, she lost what was left of her control, surrendering to the raw pleasure of it all. The heat of his mouth and the vibrations that resonated along his tongue as he lapped and suckled at her flesh was all too much. Too perfect.

She came harder than she had in her life, and while she was still shuddering with the force of that release, Rage got to his feet, settled himself behind her, and drove himself deep.

Strong hands gripped her hips, holding her in place as he claimed her with bruising thrusts. Time slowed, every moment drawn out as the pleasure amplified until it filled her awareness.

As they fucked, her new marks tingled, adding another layer of sensation to the experience. When Rage's cock swelled again, she knew what to expect, taking one last deep breath before his orgasm hit and sent them both tumbling into a glorious freefall that ended with the two of them sprawled over the edge of the bed in boneless, sated, harmony.

It took her a while to find the threads of her thoughts again and longer still to weave those threads into something substantial enough to be called a plan. By then, they'd showered, eaten, and had the ship create some clothes for Rage. He didn't think much of them, but she'd convinced him to don the pants after explaining that nudity was not acceptable among many cultures, including the ones they needed to contact.

"I still don't understand how this will help. We need an army. Warships. You said this person is not a fighter," Rage said. They were standing in front of a blank vid-screen, waiting for someone to respond to her outgoing call.

"He's not. He's something better."

She caught his hand and squeezed it. "Trust me."

He snarled something under his breath, too soft for her to hear the words.

"I know. Trust doesn't come easy for you. I get it. But this is the best shot we have."

He gave her a look that was somewhere between frustration and awe. She loved the way it made her feel to have a man like him look at her that way.

"Do this and then we'll have two weeks to ourselves. Sound good?"

He drew her hand over his crotch, letting her feel exactly how he felt about that. Yeah, she couldn't wait either.

The screen flickered to life, showing them the square-jawed visage of the only friend she trusted further than she could punt a fantra. "Raju. How's the universe treating you?"

"I'm human, so you know how it's going. Bad pay, no chance at promotion, and no fame or glory to be had. You?"

She grinned and tugged at Rage's hand, drawing him

9

MAYHEM

Bysshe brought the evening meal to Mayhem's cell himself, a clear warning to brace for bad news.

The rarely heard sounds of weapons fire earlier, followed by the ground-shaking thunder of the missile batteries launching already had him on edge. Something had happened, but he and the others had been locked down for hours. Normally the bots or Bysshe would have come by to share at least a little information, but today, they'd heard nothing.

Now the android stood outside the bars of his cell, his face as expressionless as ever.

Mayhem stopped pacing and stood across from him, hands at his sides, eyes lowered just enough to appease any verexi that might be watching.

Bysshe nodded once. "Hello, Subject Two. Before I deliver your repast, I have been ordered to convey the following information. Several hours ago, Subject One attempted to escape. He was captured and confined. At this time, it was determined that Subject One had proven to be a nonviable candidate for further study. He was scheduled for termination and informed of his change in status."

"Not long after this information was provided to him, Subject One escaped again. This time, he endangered the entire installation by attempting to depart on a computer-piloted cargo freighter. Both he and the freighter were destroyed. Any more attempts to escape will result in the immediate termination of the subject involved."

Bysshe set the tray down on the floor and stepped back to make room for a small bot to push the tray through the bars and into Mayhem's cell. He ignored both meal and bot. Instead, he gripped the bars with both hands, threw back his head, and roared. One by one, the others joined him, lifting their voices together in an act of collective grief. It would be the only time they'd be permitted to mourn together. Their captors feared them too much to let them gather in numbers greater than three, and even that was rare these days.

He wanted to fight and rail against the news, to have it be some kind of cruel new experiment meant to test him and the others. He looked at Bysshe, hoping for some small sign that this wasn't happening. That Rage still lived.

The android only stood there, his foot scuffing softly on the hard floor. It took Mayhem's grief-clouded mind a moment to recognize the message. "Be careful. Danger high for all."

He moved over to the tray, dragging one foot slightly in answer. "Understood." Then he bent down, waiting until his face was hidden before subvocalizing his question. "Did you see it happen?"

Bysshe replied in the same low undertones, his lips not moving. "No. I..." He paused for a moment before continuing. "If I did, it has been wiped from my memory. They suspected I might have helped in the second escape. They tore through my database. It is... damaged."

Mayhem kept his eyes on the chunks of meat resting on his tray. He should stop subvocalizing and let Bysshe continue his rounds. The others wouldn't know who they were mourning for... though they'd likely have guessed. He stood, balancing the tray in one hand, and looked at Bysshe. The android had told him all he could.

"May the All-Seeing Ones have mercy on his soul," he intoned the empty words of the verexi faith. They meant nothing to him, but he knew Bysshe would understand the message. They'd both lost a friend today.

"May the All-Seeing Ones have mercy on all our souls." Bysshe's voice dropped to a whisper on the last few words, and Mayhem's blood turned to ice.

It was as clear a warning as the android could give. They were running out of time.

Rage hadn't been able to find a way to free them. Now he was gone, and it was Mayhem's turn to fight.

10

RAGE

Two WEEKS alone with Mercy hadn't been enough. He could spend a lifetime exploring the pleasures of her flesh and another one discovering that there was more to life than he'd ever imagined. It wasn't all unending suffering and imprisonment. It could be funny, or pleasurable, or humbling—sometimes all three at once. His time with Mercy showed him how much he didn't know about the universe or the people living in it. She was a source of constant fascination for him. She taught him about pleasure, and patience, and how one could enhance the other. She knew so much about so many things, and her knowledge only added fuel to the hunger that always burned when she was near him.

The quiet times after their lovemaking were almost as good as the sex that came before. They'd talk and make plans, and he discovered the joy of having someone to rely on, someone who understood how to make things work in their favor.

The more he learned, the more questions he had. Were

others out there like him, more test subjects in other labs? Where had the verexi found the genetic material to create him and the rest of his clan? Could he bring his brothers somewhere so they could live free? That's all he wanted... right after he'd killed the ones who had done this to them.

Mercy didn't approve of the last part of his plan, but he would convince her eventually. He looked forward to learning how many orgasms that would require. He hoped it was a lot.

"We're about to transit back to normal space. You ready?" Mercy asked without looking at him.

"Ready." Not that he had much to do. The gunner's chair was too small for him to sit in, so they'd removed it. He was crouched over the controls, anxious to see what, and who, waited for them.

The *Timeless Blue* might not have much firepower, but what little it did have was primed and ready to fire in one of six pre-programmed barrages designed to give them a chance to escape. His job was to determine which program to initiate.

The odds were decent but only because the verexi weren't much for warfare. Mercy had explained to him that the species who had created him were so frail they had never adapted well to space travel. The radiation, variable gravity, and even the high g-forces that came with combat were more than their bodies could handle. They were too weak to fight on land, too. They were a vulnerable species trapped inside their own planetary system for the most part. That fit with what he'd learned from Bysshe about his purpose. The verexi had created the fa'rel to be the soldiers their own species could never be.

That decision was about to bite them in the ass.

They dropped into normal space, the ship groaning in protest at the abuse while the inertial dampeners struggled to keep up with the sudden stop. Now he understood why Mercy had insisted on rigging a harness for him. He hadn't wanted to be restrained, but now he could see the reason. With no chair to sit on, he needed something to keep him steady and close to the controls. If he punched his claws into anything here, he could cripple the ship.

"Shit!" Mercy's hands flew as she keyed in new commands. The monitors filled with images of other ships and his console marked them with colored dots to indicate which were friendly. Few were friends out there.

Only one verexi ship was present. It was smaller than the others, little more than a box attached to an engine. Mercy had warned him this was likely. The scrawnies couldn't travel this far, but they could send a drone ship that would allow them to be present at this moment via communication relays.

"You're sure the drone isn't armed?" he asked.

"If they are, they're in deep trouble. All these assholes don't agree on many things, but weaponizing drones and bots is at the top of the "do it and die" list."

The *assholes* she referred to were the governments of the various species and factions that lived in this part of the galaxy. They were the real threat here, not his former captors. Survival now hinged on how many of the verexi's well-bribed allies were present and whether they could be discouraged from getting involved.

They all hung in the vast empty expanse, comms silent, waiting. He felt like he'd aged a year before the comm channel chimed, announcing an incoming message. Mercy opened a link and a second later a booming voice filled the cockpit.

"This is Commander Velto Bray, representing the Galactic Legion, hailing the occupants of the *Timeless Blue*. You have a wanted fugitive aboard your vessel. As per the ratified agreement covering this area of space, your ship will be boarded and impounded until our investigation is complete."

"Last time I checked, humans hadn't been invited to sign that agreement," Mercy muttered to herself. She had warned him this might happen, and he made a note to reward her brilliance with more orgasms later.

"Doesn't matter which part of the Gal-Leg finds us, they're all the same," she'd told him during their preparations. "Self-aggrandizing idiots who care more about appearances than actually doing anything useful. If they wanted to, they could have protected my species. They didn't. Asking for help won't work. We're going to try something else."

Rage could tell this particular legion idiot was logaran. He didn't know much about them except that they were one of the more dangerous species around, with blue-black skin and bulbous features as ugly as they were distinctive.

Rage's hand hovered over the controls as he waited for events to unfold. Mercy's plan could work. But if it didn't, the two of them would go down fighting. Better a quick death now than anything the verexi would offer them later.

Mercy turned in her chair and leaned over to brush her fingertips across his lower back. "If we live through the next five minutes, I've got something I need to tell you."

"Then tell me now." He looked over at her. She grinned and shook her head.

"Nope. If you want to know, you have to stay alive. Deal?"

He nodded and uttered a low growl he knew would arouse and amuse her. "Deal."

"Okay then. Let's give the nice commander our reply." She faced forward, squared her shoulders, and started broadcasting.

"Commander Bray. This is Mercy Johnson, captain of the *Timeless Blue*. Your information is incorrect. I do not have a wanted fugitive aboard."

She paused just long enough for the commander to try speaking and then cut him off by boosting her signal so it trampled his and swamped every signal in the area. "I have a survivor on board who requests asylum from the Galactic Legion. In exchange, he will testify against his abusers, the verexi. He and his entire species have been imprisoned and experimented on continuously for decades, and it is time the verexi answered for their crimes."

Chaos followed. The verexi drone ship was bombarded with tightbeam messages. The *Blue's* comm unit almost flash-fried itself as a torrent of requests for more information poured in, and several of the ships allied to the verexi broke formation to leave the immediate area. They had no way to know what the verexi were saying, but the sheer volume of comms traffic hitting the ship was enough to light up the screen.

Mercy muted her mic but held her expression and body still as she waited for the chaos to ebb. The only part of her that moved were her feet, which were tapping out a happy little tune well out of camera view. This was going according to plan.

"Three, two, one... and there he goes, right on time," Mercy crowed as Raju's perfectly chiseled features appeared on her monitor, his signal boosted high enough to cut through the chatter.

"This is Raju Asan from GNN on the scene of a standoff between the Galactic Legion and a ship the verexi claim is carrying a dangerous fugitive. The ship in question has just countered with a claim that the verexi have tortured and experimented on the fugitive and the rest of his race."

Three windows appeared on the wall behind Raju, each one showing a different person. The first was a verexi, their dull green skin so pale it was nearly translucent. In the next was Commander Bray, and in the third was Mercy, looking determined and calm.

She was beautiful, and the idea that this amazing female would fight for him and his brothers still filled him with awe. She was the one good thing the universe had given him, and he was grateful to this delicate, fierce beauty whose body was made to sheathe his cock.

The second this was over, he'd take her right here in the cockpit, maybe tangle her up in the harness she'd made for him. Yes. That's exactly what he'd do. And if these were their last moments of life, he'd track her down and fuck her in the next life... whatever that turned out to be. He'd never given much thought to that until now, but Mercy had changed that, too. She was his forever, and not even death would change that.

On the screen, Raju was still talking, peppering the verexi with questions and then pivoting to demand what

Bray's side was going to do to make things right. Mercy stayed quiet until Raju finally asked her a direct question.

"Captain Johnson, can you prove any of the allegations you made here today?" Raju asked. This was it—the moment they'd prepped for over the last two weeks.

Mercy shook her head with a small smile. "I can't. But I'd like to introduce you to someone who can."

She turned toward him and whispered softly, "Your five minutes is up. So here's what I needed to tell you." She grinned and then winked at him. "I love you."

Before he could process her startling confession, she activated the camera at his station and introduced him. "This is Rage, formally known as Subject One. He can tell you everything you need to know."

He wanted to howl to the stars that Mercy loved him and that all was well in the universe. He also wanted to reach through the screen and throttle the verexi until its soulless black eyes popped, but instead he kept his eyes on the image of Mercy and told his story. It wasn't the revenge he'd always dreamed of, but killing the enemy would not free his brothers.

This might.

And once he was done, he was going to tie Mercy down and tell her he loved her too.

11

MAYHEM

THE VEREXI HAD NEVER SHOWN him a moment's kindness before, which made Mayhem doubt everything the scrawnies were saying now. Nothing was the same after Rage's death. There were no more experiments or medical tests. He'd been pain free for weeks, and for the first time in memory, he had enough time and rest to heal and grow strong.

Bysshe had no information to share, and as the days dragged on, Mayhem grew increasingly concerned.

Something had changed, but what?

The answer came eventually, but it wasn't what Mayhem had expected.

"You are to be freed." Bysshe's announcement had stunned him into complete silence.

"Freed? They're letting us out of our cells?" he asked.

"The verexi have ended this experiment and decommissioned the base. As you cannot survive here without support, you will be moved to an uninhabited planet. You will be given supplies and allowed to live the rest of your lives in peace. Follow me, Subject Two. You are to depart immediately."

Ten minutes later, his entire clan stepped into the hold of a transport ship. They stayed silent and still, not even daring to subvocalize until the doors closed and the distant rumble of an engine made the entire deck thrum.

"Seat yourself quickly and strap in. This vessel is fully automated and will launch in sixty seconds, whether you are secured or not." Bysshe made a point of taking a seat on one of the benches that lined the sides of the space and strapping in. They all followed suit.

Mayhem sat next to the android, who immediately scuffed his foot in the familiar "danger" message.

So, this wasn't over. Mayhem almost felt relieved. The others looked at him expectantly. They hadn't believed this was an act of kindness, either.

Once the engine noise had died away a little, he cleared his throat and subvocalized to Bysshe. "What's really going on?"

Instead of answering, the android unclipped his harness and rose. He walked over to a keypad near the front of the hold and tapped out a long string of characters. "Now, we can talk. I've disabled the remote monitoring system the verexi are using to watch you. We haven't got long before they notice, so I will be brief."

Everyone leaned forward, gold and amber eyes fixed on Bysshe, the only ally they'd ever had. "Something happened. I do not know what it is. They have altered my programming somehow to prevent me from learning about it or retaining any information I may inadvertently acquire. The block did not prevent me from discovering what they planned to do in the future. They intend to vent the atmosphere from this section just before we arrive at the planet. Once you are dead, the ship will crash, destroying all evidence. If you want to live, we have one chance. We have to commandeer this ship and maintain control long enough to land."

"Killing us, I understand. But why destroy this ship and the bots running it? Why kill you?" Strife asked. He'd always had a sharp mind and a way of cutting to the heart of things.

Bysshe touched his bald temple. "They suspect I have been helping you and have done invasive examinations of my memory banks trying to find proof. I was able to delete or hide most of the evidence, but it is apparent that I am a liability to them. So are all of you. They are willing to sacrifice this ship in order to make your deaths believable."

"Then we should take this ship and go," Menace said, his voice sharp and full of anger.

"If we run, they will hunt us. This ship has no weapons and no communications system." Bysshe looked down at him. "We have one chance."

Mayhem nodded, unclipped his harness, and rose to stand beside the android. "Then we do what Rage always told us to do if the opportunity came. We rise up. We fight. We win." He raised his fist into the air and roared.

The others joined him, and in that moment, Mayhem could almost feel the presence of the one who should have been here to enjoy this moment.

"For Rage!" he called out, and the others echoed his cry.

It was time to fight back.

Finally.

EPILOGUE—MERCY

NO PLAN SURVIVED IMPLEMENTATION. She and Rage knew that better than most. That knowledge didn't help them deal with the catastrophic clusterfuck they were watching unfold on the planet below.

They stood together in the cockpit of the *Blue,* leaning into each other as they tried to figure out what the fuck had gone wrong with their plan to free the rest of the fa'rel.

Things had been going so well, both with the verexi and between the two of them. She felt like someone had installed new batteries in her soul. Rage was wild, and raw, and real, and his energy filled her—not just in bed but in every waking moment. The *Blue* rang with laughter for the first time in years. It had been good. Until now.

Now, it was a disaster.

More data filled the screen, all of it bad news. Rage slammed his fist into the nearest bulkhead, adding another dent to the interior. With so many of them now, she'd stopped complaining about them. Besides, not all the damage was his fault. She'd torn loose a few chunks of the ship herself during their marathon sexcapades. She hadn't worried about it since the plan had been to join the rest of Rage's clan on the surface and only use the *Blue* as an emergency escape vehicle.

That plan had gone to the hells in nine rocket-powered handcarts.

Instead of releasing their prisoners on an uninhabited planet as agreed, the verexi had tried to kill them all. At least, that's the only reason Rage could think of that would trigger his brothers to rebel and bring down the ship they traveled on. The verexi weren't talking, his brothers were trapped on the surface, and the ship along with the plan lay in ruins.

"I want to join them," Rage said to the male on his screen. Another officer from the legion, this man sported crimson mandibles and an exoskeleton of black chiton.

"You cannot." Her translator knew the alien's language well enough to get most points across, but it wasn't perfect.

She could tell that much because either the liksik species took a long damned time to say anything, or it was paraphrasing because those two words had been translated from nearly a dozen clicks and popping sounds.

"They were supposed to be freed!" Rage snarled, and she reached out to take his hand with hers. He caught her fingers as he always did, running one claw over the pattern on her wrist. He knew what that did to her, but she'd rather get all hot and bothered than let her mate lose his temper.

"You said they were nonviolent!" the officer retorted.

That wasn't what Rage had said at all. She'd been there for every conversation. He'd promised that his brothers could learn to be peaceful citizens of the Galactic Legion given enough time and the means to make a life for themselves. He'd also warned them that the verexi would try something, but the ones with the power hadn't believed him. The verexi didn't have an army, but their system held vast amounts of talium-6, a precious, crystalline mineral that powered every star drive in existence. They'd used that to negotiate, twisting the truth until there were enough doubts to let them escape serious repercussions. Hells, they'd even convinced the others that Rage shouldn't be allowed to contact his clan until they were safely on the surface. They had no idea what the verexi had told his brothers about him or their future.

Now, they couldn't even find out what happened on board, because the only witnesses were verexi-controlled bots. The assholes had planned this... and it had worked.

Mostly.

According to the scans, the ship had crashed surprisingly close to where their supplies had been soft-landed. Better yet, life signs proved that everyone on board had survived the crash. Rage's brothers were safe.

"I need to get down there," Rage repeated.

The officer paused, listening to something being said off screen. Then he said, "That's not possible. This planet is within the boundaries of the verexi empire. They have denied you permission to land. In fact, they are requesting that I transfer to your ship and personally escort you out of their territory. All permissions and licenses to access their space have been terminated, effective immediately."

Mercy scowled at the screen. "If you leave your post, no one will be left to observe what happens. You have orders to ensure that this transfer went according to plan. To do that, you have to stay with the verexi and ensure nothing happens to the fa'rel. That's your *job!*" And as far as she was concerned, the officer had failed miserably at it.

Rage leaned in and flashed his fangs at the officer. "They don't even know I'm here. I wasn't allowed to make contact until they landed. I need to talk to them. Now."

The liksik showed the slightest hesitation before answering. "It's impossible. The ship's communications are down. We have no way to reach them."

"Then let us *land!*" Rage's roar shook the deck under her feet, but she already knew it was a wasted effort. The verexi didn't want anyone else on that planet. No witnesses meant no chance of their secret getting out. Whatever those secrets were...

The officer looked lost now, his mandibles clattering together in what looked like agitation. "You need to leave this area immediately."

"And my clan?" Rage demanded.

The liksik officer muted the channel while he had another, more prolonged conversation with someone off screen. When he spoke again, he sounded more certain. "They'll be safe. This system is now restricted space. No one in. No one out. A defense grid will be placed around the planet and warning beacons will be posted. Your clan has their planet, as agreed."

"The hells they do. They're still prisoners!" Even before she opened her mouth, Mercy knew she couldn't change anything. The decisions were already made. The verexi had cut a deal with someone, and they had no time to figure out who it was or how to counter them. Public outrage had burned in their favor for a while, but the news cycle had already moved on to the next story.

The officer started clicking and popping again, and she knew what he'd say before the translation started. "This incident will need to be reviewed at a higher level. You will be contacted and invited to submit your statement in writing at a later time."

They'd just been dumped into diplomatic limbo. *Fuck.*

The air around Rage almost crackled with barely repressed fury and frustration. "I'm not leaving until I speak to them. They don't even know I'm alive."

"If you do not leave immediately, you will be in violation of the terms of this agreement," the liksik chittered, his appendages all quivering in agitation.

Mercy moved before Rage could. "We'll go," she said tersely and then disconnected the link with a slap of her hand.

"No!"

She turned and took hold of Rage's horns, wrapping her fingers around the part that curled beside his jaw. "Yes. We're going. For now. We can't fight this. We don't have the money or the connections to fix this fuckery."

"I'm not leaving them."

She smiled and kept up the gentle stroking. *"We're* not leaving them. Humans have a saying that I think you need to learn."

"Hmm?" he was nuzzling her hand now, his amber eyes already filling with heat.

"He who fights and then runs away..." she started.

"Is a coward!" Rage snapped.

"No. They live to fight another day. Your clan are safe

for now. We'll find a way to help them eventually. I promise. This fight isn't over." She pulled his head down and kissed him. "But first, we need a plan."

"Does this plan include vengeance and copious amounts of sex?"

She threw back her head and laughed. "As a matter of fact, it does."

She took her seat and fired up the engines, charting a course for the edge of verexi space. That was when she noticed a small blue light flashing on her comm console. Someone had sent her a data packet. She called up the log, but what she saw there made no sense. According to her system, it had been sent the day she'd first met Rage. But that was weeks ago. Why hadn't it registered until now?

She scanned it for anything dangerous, but it was exactly what it appeared to be, a simple data packet. Once they were underway, she called Rage over so they could review it together. Something told her this would be about him.

She was right.

The recording was audio only, but she recognized the voice right away as Bysshe, the android from the lunar installation.

"Hello, Captain Johnson. This is Bysshe, and this message was recorded before you were out of range of the lunar outpost. It had a time delay, which means that it is now several weeks past the day we last spoke. I apologize for the delay, but it was necessary.

"The verexi suspect I was complicit in the escape of Subject One. To protect myself and the other fa'rel, I am purging my data banks of all memory of his escape as well as any other incriminating information I had obtained during my time here. I'm sending it to you in hopes you will share it with Subject One."

The recording lapsed into silence for a second. "Though I suppose he'll be calling himself Rage now. Hello, Rage. I hope you are well and thriving. I will continue to protect your clan as best I can. They are strong and determined to survive, just as you are. Did you know that fa'rel is a verexi word? It means wild ones in one of their older dialects. But that is not the name of your species. I can't tell you what it was. There's no mention of it that I can find, but I do know that you were not created by the verexi. You and the others were abducted and altered, but your species is out there, on a planet in one of the unknown areas of the universe. I have sent you all the information I could find, but to find them you will have to cross several contested areas and violate the legion's non-interference pact with still-developing races."

Rage snarled, which was actually a pretty mild reaction considering what they'd just discovered.

Mercy had been explaining the complex rules that governed the Galactic Legion, and he'd learned enough to know that what Bysshe was suggesting wouldn't be easy.

"The verexi will do all they can to hide the truth of what they've done. I will do what I can to protect your clan, but I don't have enough information to prove anything, and the verexi have powerful allies. You will need to find your people, Rage. And you must hurry. Be well, and good luck. I hope to see you again someday."

The message ended.

For the first time in her life, she was grateful that

humanity had never been invited to sign on with the legion. She wasn't bound by their rules... and neither was Rage.

They could do this. Humans might not rule the stars, but they did one thing better than any other species she'd encountered. They persisted. And she could do better than merely endure. Now that she had Rage in her bed, with all his youthful fire and a stubbornness the equal of her own, she could do more. They'd both been survivors before they met. Now that they had each other, anything was possible.

"Give me a big enough lever and I will move worlds," she murmured against his lips.

His laughter rumbled up from his chest. "I am big enough to rock your world, little female." He set a big hand on her shoulder. "How do we find them?"

His trust in her was like a shot of premium narcotics straight to the bloodstream. "I call some friends. Cash in more favors. We make a plan." She turned and nuzzled her cheek against his fingers. "Then we go find your people."

He pulled her out of the chair and kissed her, his tongue tangling and dancing with hers until she was breathless and trembling. Stars above, the things he could do with that tongue...

They broke their embrace to watch as the fa'rels' new homeworld dwindled to a speck on the monitors, the two of them wrapped in each other's arms. "I will be back for you, my brothers. Until then, be free. Be well. Survive until I return."

"You mean until we return," she reminded him.

"Yes. We. But before I introduce you to them, I will need to speak to them all."

She rubbed her ass against the hard line of his cock, already suspecting where this was going. "Why?"

"Because they are all like me. Strong, virile males. But they are alone down there, and when they see what a magnificent mate I have found, they will want to take you for their own."

An entire clan of hot, horned, and horny alien males. Many women out there would give their life savings to find something like that. She wasn't one of them. She had all she needed. "Then I'll have to tell them I want no other male but you," she said.

"No. Then I would have to kill them. Once they are free, they can find their own females. You are mine."

She tipped her head back to smile up at him. "So you keep telling me."

"Do you doubt it?" he rumbled.

Not for a moment. She just wasn't going to give him the satisfaction of saying it aloud. "Maybe you should remind me again who I belong to."

His purr was low and deep, the sound making her pulse race and her pussy cream in anticipation. She squealed, ducked out of his arms, and pelted down the corridor to their quarters.

She wasn't going to make it. Not with a predator only a few steps behind, primed and ready to show her all the ways she belonged to him.

They were headed for danger and the unknown, looking for answers to questions they'd only just discovered ... but they'd be together. The two of them against the universe.

Bring it on.

***

Thank You for Reading Marked For Rage

I hope you enjoyed Mercy and Rage's story. Don't worry, we'll be hearing from this couple again in later books! I invite you to explore the rest of the Crashed And Claimed Series.

MARKED FOR STRIFE

**It was supposed to be the trip of a lifetime...
Now she's just trying to stay alive.**

Rissa can't believe her luck. She won an all-expenses paid trip on a luxury matchmaking cruise. She's not looking for love, but a few weeks of five-star pampering while visiting other planets sounds perfect... until it all goes wrong.

Abandoning ship wasn't on her itinerary, and neither is the growly but oh-so-sexy alien who is half convinced she's the enemy, and utterly certain she's *his*. She's got a list of the reasons they're wrong for each other, but when they're together, everything just feels right.

Crash landing on a prison planet may not be the vacation she dreamed of, but it might turn out to be the best "worst" day of her life.

**Buckle up. This sci-fi romance contains an alien with fur, fangs, horns, and a very possessive attitude when it comes to the woman he's claimed for his own.

Continue the adventure with Marked For Strife

Want to read more stories with book boyfriends
that are out of this world?

Check out Susan Hayes' other Science Fiction Romance
Series at

Susanhayes.ca

Manufactured by Amazon.ca
Bolton, ON

28211034R00120